**LIVE FR** ◁ **W9-CTJ-556**

"We'd hate to bombard your planet. Please don't compel us to."

Holm drew savagely on his cigar before he stabbed it into its smoke. "Yes, sure," he snapped. "Standard technique. Eliminate a space fleet, and its planet has to yield or you'll pound it into radioactive slag. Nice work for a man, that, hunh? Well, my colleagues and I saw this war coming years back. We knew we'd never have much of a navy by comparison, if only because you bastards have so much more population and area behind you. But defense— Admiral, you're at the end of a long line of communication and supply. We're *here*. . . .

"Okay, once in a great while, by sheer luck, you doubtless could land a warhead, and it might be big and dirty. We'd weather that, and the home guard has decontamination teams. Chances of its hitting anything important are about like drawing three for a royal flush. No ship of yours can get close enough with an energy projector husky enough to pinken a baby's bottom. But there're no size and mass limits on our ground-based photon weapons; we can use whole rivers to cool their generators while their snouts whiff you out of our sky. Now tell me why in flaming chaos we should surrender."

# PEOPLE·OF THE WIND

# POUL ANDERSON

BAEN

THE PEOPLE OF THE WIND

A Baen Book

Baen Publishing Enterprises
P.O. Box 1403
Riverdale, N.Y. 10471

ISBN: 0-671-72164-X

Cover art by Larry Schwinger

First Baen printing, April 1993

Distributed by
SIMON & SCHUSTER
1230 Avenue of the Americas
New York, N.Y. 10020

Printed in the United States of America

To *Edmond Hamilton* and *Leigh Brackett*
with thanks for many years of adventure

# I

YOU can't leave now," Daniel Holm told his son. "Any day we may be at war. We may already be."

"That's just why I have to go," the young man answered. "They're calling Khruaths about it around the curve of the planet. Where else should I fare than to my choth?"

When he spoke thus, more than his wording became bird. The very accent changed. He was no longer using the Planha-influenced Anglic of Avalon— pure vowels, r's trilled, m's and n's and ng's almost hummed, speech deepened and slowed and strongly cadenced; rather, it was as if he were trying to translate for a human listener the thought of an Ythrian brain.

1

The man whose image occupied the phone screen did not retort, "You might consider staying with your own family," as once he would have. Instead Daniel Holm nodded, and said quietly, "I see. You're not Chris now, you're Arinnian," and all at once looked old.

That wrenched at the young man. He reached forth, but his fingers were stopped by the screen. "I'm always Chris, Dad," he blurted. "It's only that I'm Arinnian too. And, and, well, if war comes, the choths will need to be prepared for it, won't they? I'm going to help—shouldn't be gone long, really."

"Sure. Good voyage."

"Give Mother and everybody my love."

"Why not call her yourself?"

"Well, uh, I do have to hurry . . . and it's not as if this were anything unusual, my heading off to the mountains, and—oh—"

"Sure," said Daniel Holm. "I'll tell them. And you give my regards to your mates." The Second Marchwarden of the Lauran System blanked off.

Arinnian turned from the instrument. For a moment he winced and bit his lip. He hated hurting people who cared about him. But why couldn't they understand? Their kind called it "going bird," being received into a choth, as if in some fashion those who did were renouncing the race that begot them. He couldn't count how many hours he had tried to make his parents—make any number of orthohumans—see that he was widening and purifying his humanity.

A bit of dialogue ran through memory: "Dad, look, two species can't inhabit the same globe for generations without pretty deep mutual consequences. Why do you go sky-hunting? Why does Ferune serve wine at his table? And those're the most superficial symptoms."

"I know that much. Credit me with some fair-mindedness, hm? Thing is, you're making a quantum jump."

"Because I'm to be a member of Stormgate? Listen,

the choths have been accepting humans for the past hundred years."

"Not in such flocks as lately. And my son wasn't one of them. I'd've ... liked to see you carry on *our* traditions."

"Who says I won't?"

"To start with, you'll not be under human law any more, you'll be under choth law and custom. . . . Hold on. That's fine, if you're an Ythrian. Chris, you haven't got the chromosomes. Those who've pretended they did, never fitted well into either race, ever again."

"Damnation, I'm not pretending—!"

Arinnian thrust the scene from him as if it were a physical thing. He was grateful for the prosaic necessities of preparation. To reach Lythran's aerie before dark, he must start soon. Of course, a car would cover the distance in less than an hour; but who wanted to fly caged in metal and plastic?

He was nude. More and more, those who lived like him were tending to discard clothes altogether and use skin paint for dress-up. But everybody sometimes needed garments. An Ythrian, too, was seldom without a belt and pouch. This trip would get chilly, and he lacked feathers. He crossed the tiny apartment to fetch coverall and boots.

Passing, he glanced at the desk whereon lay papers of his work and, in a heap, the texts and references he was currently employing, printouts from Library Central. *Blast!* he thought. *I loathe quitting when I've nearly seen how to prove that theorem.*

In mathematics he could soar. He often imagined that then his mind knew the same clean ecstasy an Ythrian, aloft alone, must know in the flesh. Thus he had been willing to accept the compromise which reconciled him and his father. He would continue his studies, maintain his goal of becoming a professional mathematician. To this end, he would accept some financial help, though he would no longer be expected to live at home. The rest of what little income he required he would earn himself, as herdsman and hunter when he went off to be among the Ythrians.

Daniel Holm had growled, through the hint of a grin, "You own a good mind, son. I didn't want to see it go to waste. At the same time, it's too good. If 'tweren't for your birding, you'd be so netted in your books, when you aren't drawing a picture or writing a poem, you'd never get any exercise; at last your bottom would grow fast to your chair, and you'd hardly notice. I s'pose I should feel a little grateful to your friends for making their kind of athlete out of you."

"My chothmates," Arinnian corrected him. He had just been given his new name and was full of glory and earnestness. That was four years ago; today he could smile at himself. The guv'nor had not been altogether wrong.

Thus at thirty—Avalonian reckoning—Christopher Holm was tall, slender, but wide-shouldered. In features as well as build, he took after his mother: long head, narrow face, thin nose and lips, blue eyes, mahogany hair (worn short in the style of those who do much gravbelt flying), and as yet not enough beard to be worth anything except regular applications of antigrowth enzyme. His complexion, naturally fair, was darkened by exposure. Laura, a G5 star, has only 72 percent the luminosity of Sol and less ultraviolet light in proportion; but Avalon, orbiting at a mean distance of 0.81 astronomical unit in a period of 0.724 Terran, gets 10 percent more total irradiation than man evolved under.

He made the customary part-by-part inspection of his unit before he put arms through straps and secured buckle at waist. The twin cone-pointed cylinders on his back had better have fully charged accumulators and fully operating circuits. If not, he was dead. One Ythrian couldn't hold back a human from toppling out of the sky. A couple of times, several together had effected a rescue; but those were herders, carrying lassos which they could cast around their comrade and pull on without getting in each other's way. You dared not count on such luck. O God, to have real wings!

He donned a leather helmet and lowered the goggles which were his poor substitute for a nictitating membrane. He sheathed knife and slugthrower at his hips. There would be nothing of danger—no chance of a duel being provoked, since a Khruath was peaceholy—not that deathpride quarrels ever happened often—but the Stormgate folk were mostly hunters and didn't leave their tools behind. He had no need to carry provisions. Those would be supplied from the family stores, to which he contributed his regular share, and ferried to the rendezvous on a gravsled.

Going out the door, he found himself on ground level. Humans had ample room on Avalon—about ten million of them; four million Ythrians—and even here in Gray, the planet's closest approximation to a real city, they built low and widespread. A couple of highrises sufficed for resident or visiting ornithoids.

Arinnian flicked controls. Negaforce thrust him gently, swiftly upward. Leveling off, he spent a minute savoring the view.

The town sprawled across hills green with trees and susin, color-patched with gardens, that ringed Falkayn Bay. Upon the water skimmed boats; being for pleasure, they were principally sail-driven hydrofoils. A few cargo vessels, long shapes of functional grace, lay at the docks, loaded and unloaded by assorted robots. One was coming in, from Brendan's Islands to judge by the course, and one was standing out to the Hesperian Sea, which flared silver where the sun struck it and, elsewhere, ran sapphire till it purpled on northern and southern horizons.

Laura hung low in the empty west, deeper aureate than at midday. The sky was a slowly darkening blue; streaks of high cirrus clouds, which Arinnian thought of as breastfeathers, promised fair weather would continue. A salt breeze whispered and cooled his cheeks.

Air traffic was scant. Several Ythrians passed by, wings gleaming bronze and amber. A couple of humans made beltflights like Arinnian; distant, they were hardly to be told from a flock of slim leathery draculas which evening had drawn out of some cave. More humans rode in cars, horizontal raindrops that flung back the light with inanimate fierceness. Two or three vans lumbered along and an intercontinental liner was settling toward the airport. But Gray was never wildly busy.

High up, however, paced shapes that had not been seen here since the end of the Troubles: warcraft on patrol.

*War against the Terran Empire*— Shivering, Arinnian lined out eastward, inland.

Already he could see his destination, far off beyond the coastal range and the central valley, like a cloudbank on worldedge, those peaks which were the highest in Corona, on all Avalon if you didn't count Oronesia. Men called them the Andromedas, but in his Anglic Arinnian had also taken to using the Planha name, Weathermother.

Ranchland rolled beneath him. Here around Gray, the mainly Ythrian settlements northward merged with the mainly human south; both ecologies blent with Avalon's own, and the country became a checkerboard. Man's grainfields, ripening as summer waned, lay tawny amidst huge green pastures where Ythrians grazed their maukh and mayaw. Stands of timberwood, oak or pine, windnest or hammerbranch, encroached on nearly treeless reaches of berylline native susin where you might still glimpse an occasional barysauroid. The rush of his passage blew away fretfulness. Let the Empire attack the Domain ... if it dared! Meanwhile he, Arinnian, was bound for Eyath—for his whole choth, of course, and oneness with it, but chiefly he would see Eyath again.

Across the dignity of the dining hall, a look passed between them. *Shall we wander outside and be our-selves?* She asked permission to leave of her father Lythran and her mother Blawsa; although she was their dependent, that was mere ritual, yet rituals mattered greatly. In like fashion Arinnian told the younger persons among whom he was benched that he had the wish of being unaccompanied. He and Eyath left side by side. It caused no break in the slow, silence-punctuated conversation wherein everyone else took part. Their closeness went back to their childhood and was fully accepted.

The compound stood on a plateau of Mount Far-view. At the middle lifted the old stone tower which housed the senior members of the family and their children. Lower wooden structures, on whose sod roofs bloomed amberdragon and starbells, were for the unwed and for retainers and their kin. Further down a slope lay sheds, barns, and mews. The whole could not be seen at once from the ground, because Ythrian trees grew among the buildings: braidbark, copperwood, gaunt lightningrod, jewelleaf which sheened beneath the moon and by day would shimmer irides-cent. The flowerbeds held natives, more highly evolved than anything from offplanet—sweet small janie, pungent livewell, graceful trefoil and Buddha's cup, a harp vine which the breeze brought ever so faintly to singing. Otherwise the night was quiet and, at this altitude, cold. Breath smoked white.

Eyath spread her wings. They were more slender than average, though spanning close to six meters. This naturally forced her to rest on hands and tail. "Br-r-r!" she laughed. "Hoarfrost. Let's lift." In a crack and whirl of air, she rose.

"You forgot," he called. "I've taken off my belt."

She settled on a platform built near the top of a copperwood. Ythrians made few redundant noises; obviously he could climb. He thought she overrated his skill, merely because he was better at it than she. A misstep in that murky foliage could bring a nasty fall. But he couldn't refuse the implicit challenge and keep her respect. He gripped a branch, chinned himself up, and groped and rustled his way.

Ahead, he heard her murmur to the uhoth which had fluttered along behind her. It brought down game with admirable efficiency, but he felt she made too much fuss over it. Well, no denying she was husband-high. He didn't quite like admitting that to himself. (*Why?* he wondered fleetingly.)

When he reached the platform, he saw her at rest on feet and alatans, the uhoth on her right wrist while her left hand stroked it. Morgana, almost full, stood dazzling white over the eastward sierra and made the plumes of Eyath glow. Her crest was silhouetted against the Milky Way. Despite the moon, constellations glistered through upland air, Wheel, Swords, Zirraukh, vast sprawling Ship. . . .

He sat down beside her, hugging his knees. She made the small ululation which expressed her gladness at his presence. He responded as best he could. Above the clean curve of her muzzle, the great eyes glimmered.

Abruptly she broke off. He followed her gaze and saw a new star swing into heaven. "A guardian satellite?" she asked. Her tone wavered the least bit.

"What else?" he replied. "I think it must be the latest one they've orbited."

"How many by now?"

"They're not announcing that," he reminded her. Ythrians always had trouble grasping the idea of government secrets. Of government in any normal human sense, for that matter. Marchwardens Ferune and Holrn had been spending more energy in getting the choths to cooperate than in actual defense preparations. "My father doesn't believe we can have too many."

"The wasted wealth—"

"Well, if the Terrans come—"

"Do you expect they will?"

The trouble he heard brought his hand to squeeze her, very gently, on the neck, and afterward run fingers along her crest. Her feathers were warm, smooth and yet infinitely textured. "I don't know," he said. "Maybe they can settle the border question peacefully. Let's hope." The last two words were perforce in Anglic rather than Planha. Ythrians had never beseeched the future. She too was bilingual, like every educated colonist.

His look went back skyward. Sol lay . . . yonder in the Maukh, about where four stars formed the horns . . . how far? Oh, yes, 205 light-years. He recalled reading that, from there, Quetlan and Laura were in a constellation called the Lupus. None of the three suns had naked-eye visibility across such an abyss. They were mere G-type dwarfs; they merely happened to be circled by some motes which had fermented till there were chemistries that named those motes Terra, Ythri, Avalon, and loved them.

"Lupus," he mused. "An irony."

Eyath whistled: "?"

He explained, adding: "The lupus is, or was, a beast of prey on Terra. And to us, Sol lies in the sign of a big, tame herd animal. But who's attacking whom?"

"I haven't followed the news much," she said, low and not quite steadily. "It seemed a fog only, to me or mine. What need we reck if others clashed? Then all of a sudden— Might we have caused some of the trouble, Arinnian? Could folk of ours have been too rash, too rigid?"

Her mood was so uncharacteristic, not just of Ythrian temperament in general but of her usually

sunny self, that astonishment jerked his head around.
"What's made you this anxious?" he asked.

Her lips nuzzled the uhoth, as if seeking consolation
that he thought he could better give. Its beak preened
her. He barely heard: "Vodan."

"What? Oh! Are you betrothed to Vodan?"

His voice had cracked. *Why am I shaken?* he wondered. *He's a fine fellow. And of this same choth, too;
no problems of changed law and custom, culture
shock, homesickness—* Arinnian's glance swept over
the Stormgate country. Above valleys steep-walled,
dark and fragrant with woods, snowpeaks lifted. Closer
was a mountainside down which a waterfall stood pil-
larlike under the moon. A night-flying bugler sounded
its haunting note through stillness. On the Plains of
Long Reach, in arctic marshes, halfway around the
planet on a scorching New Gaiilan savannah, amidst
the uncounted islands that made up most of what dry
land Avalon had—how might she come to miss the
realm of her choth?

*No, wait, I'm thinking like a human. Ythrians get
around more. Eyath's own mother is from the Sagittarius basin, often goes back to visit. . . . Why shouldn't I
think like a human? I am one. I've found wisdom,
rightness, happiness of a sort in certain Ythrian ways;
but no use pretending I'll ever be an Ythrian, ever wed
a winged girl and dwell in our own aerie.*

She was saying: "Well, no, not exactly. Galemate,
do you believe I wouldn't tell you of my betrothal or
invite you to my wedding feast? But he is a . . . a
person I've grown very fond of. You know I planned
on staying single till my studies were finished." She
wanted the difficult, honored calling of musician.
"Lately . . . well, I thought about it a lot during my
last lovetime. I grew hotter then than ever before, and
I kept imagining Vodan."

Arinnian felt himself flush. He stared at the remote
gleam of a glacier. She shouldn't tell him such things.

It wasn't decent. An unmarried female Ythrian, or one whose husband was absent, was supposed to stay isolated from males when the heat came upon her; but she was also supposed to spend the energy it raised in work, or study, or meditation, or—

Eyath sensed his embarrassment. Her laughter rippled and she laid a hand over his. The slim fingers, the sharp claws gripped him tenderly. "Why, I declare you're shocked! What for?"

"You wouldn't talk like that to—your father, a brother—" *And you shouldn't feel that way, either. Never. Estrus or no. Lonely, maybe; dreamy, yes; but not like some sweating trull in the bed of some cheap hotel room. Not you, Eyath.*

"True, it'd be improper talk in Stormgate. I used to wonder if I shouldn't marry into a less strict choth. Vodan, though— Anyhow, Arinnian, dear, I can tell you anything. Can't I?"

"Yes." *After all, I'm not really an Ythrian.*

"We discussed it later, he and I," she said. "Marriage, I mean. No use denying, children would be a terrible handicap at this stage. But we fly well together; and our parents have been nudging us for a long time, it'd be so good an alliance between houses. We've wondered if, maybe, if we stayed hriccal the first few years—"

"That doesn't work too well, does it?" he said as her voice trailed off, through the bloodbeat in his ears. "That is, uh, continual sex relations may not be how Ythrians reinforce pair bonds, but that doesn't mean sex has no importance. If you separate every lovetime, you, you, well, you're rejecting each other, aren't you? Why not, uh, contraception?"

"No."

He knew why her race, almost if not quite uniformly, spurned that. Children—the strong parental instinct of both mates—*were* what kept them together. If small wings closed around you and a small head snuggled down alongside your keelbone, you forgot the inevitable tensions and frustrations of marriage as much as if you were a human who had just happily coupled.

"We could postpone things till I've finished my studies and his business is on the wing," Eyath said. Arinnian remembered that Vodan, in partnership with various youths from Stormgate, Many Thermals, and The Tarns, had launched a silvicultural engineering firm. "But if war comes—kaah, he's in the naval reserve—"

Her free arm went around his shoulder, a blind gesture. He leaned his weight on an elbow so he could reach beneath the wings to embrace her stiff body. And he murmured to her, his sister since they both were children, what comfort he was able.

In the morning they felt more cheerful. It was not in Ythrian nature to brood—not even as a bad pun, they giving live birth—and bird-humans had tried to educate themselves out of the habit. Today, apart from a few retainers on maintenance duty, Lythran's household would fly to that mountain where the regional Khruath met. On the way they would be joined by other Stormgate families; arrived, they would find other choths entirely. However bleak the occasion of this gathering was, some of the color, excitement, private business, and private fun would be there that pervaded the regular assemblies.

And the dawn was clear and a tailwind streamed.

A trumpet called. Lythran swung from the top of his tower. Folk lifted their wings until the antlibranch slits beneath stood agape, purple from blood under the oxygen-drinking tissues. The wings clapped back down, and back on high; the Ythrians thundered off the ground, caught an updraft, and rode it into formation. Then they flew eastward over the crags.

Arinnian steered close to Eyath. She flashed him a smile and broke into song. She had a beautiful voice—it could nearly be named soprano—which turned the skirls and gutturals of Planha into a lilt. What she cataracted forth on the air was a traditional carol, but it was for Arinnian because he had rendered it into Anglic, though he always felt that his tricks of language had failed to convey either the rapture or the vision.

"Light that leaps from a sun still sunken
hails the hunter at hover,
washes his wings in molten morning,
startles the stars to cover.
Blue is the bell of hollow heaven,
rung by a risen blowing.
Wide lie woodlands and mountain meadows,
great and green with their growing.
 But—look, oh, look!—
 a red ray struck
 through tattered mist.
 A broadhorn buck
 stands traitor-kissed.
 The talons crook.

"Tilt through tumult of wakened wind-noise.
whining, whickering, whirly;
slip down a slantwise course of currents.
Ha, but the hunt comes early!
Poise on the pinions, take the target
there in the then of swooping—
Thrust on through by a wind-wild wingbeat,
stark the stabber comes stooping.
 The buck may pose
 for one short breath
 before it runs
 from whistling death.
 The hammer stuns.
 The talons close.

"Broad and bright is the nearing noontide.
Drawn to dreamily drowsing,
shut-eyed in shade he sits now, sated.
Suddenly sounds his rousing.
Cool as the kiss of a ghost, then gusty,
rinsed by the rainfall after,
breezes brawl, and their forest fleetness
lives in leafage like laughter.
   Among the trees
   the branches shout
   and groan and throw
   themselves about.
   It's time to go.
   The talons ease.

"Beat from bough up to row through rainstreams.
Thickly thutters the thunder.
Hailwinds harried by lash of lightning
roar as they rise from under.
Blind in the black of clawing cloudbanks,
wins he his way, though slowly,
breaks their barrier, soars in sunlight.
High is heaven and holy.
   The glow slants gold
   caressingly
   across and through
   immensity
   of silent blue.
   The talons fold."

# II

AVALON rotates in 11 hours, 22 minutes, 12 seconds, on an axis tilted 21° from the normal to the orbital plane. Thus Gray, at about 43° N., knows short nights always; in summer the darkness seems scarcely a blink. Daniel Holm wondered if that was a root of his weariness.

Probably not. He was born here. His ancestors had lived here for centuries; they arrived with Falkayn. If individuals could change their circadian rhythms—as he'd had to do plenty often in his spacefaring days— surely a race could. The medics said that settling down in a gravity field only 80 percent of Terra's made more severe demands than that on the organism; its whole fluid balance and kinesthesia must readjust. Besides, what humans underwent was trivial compared to what their fellow colonists did. The Ythrians had had to shift a whole breeding cycle to a different day, year, weight, climate, diet, world. No wonder their first several generations had been of low fertility. Nevertheless, they survived; in the end, they flourished.

Therefore it was nonsense to suppose a man got tired from anything except overwork—and, yes, age, in spite of antisenescence. Or was it? Really? As you grew old, as you neared your dead and all who had gone before them, might your being not yearn back to its earliest beginnings, to a manhome you had never seen but somehow remembered?

*Crock! Come off that! Who said eighty-four is old?* Holm yanked a cigar from his pocket and snapped off the end. The inhalation which lit it was unnecessarily hard.

He was of medium height, and stocky in the olive tunic and baggy trousers worn by human members of the Ythrian armed services. The mongoloid side of his descent showed in round head, wide face, high cheekbones, a fullness about the lips and the blunt nose; the caucasoid was revealed in gray eyes, a skin that would have been pale did he not spend his free time outdoors hunting or gardening, and the hair that was grizzled on his scalp but remained crisp and black on his chest. Like most men on the planet, he suppressed his beard.

He was wading into the latest spate of communications his aides had passed on to him, when the intercom buzzed and said: "First Marchwarden Ferune wishes discussion."

"Sure!" Holm's superior was newly back from Ythri. The man reached for a two-way plate, withdrew his hand, and said, "Why not in the flesh? I'll be right there."

He stumped from his office. The corridor beyond hummed and bustled—naval personnel, civilian employees of the Lauran admiralty—and overloaded the building's air system till the odors of both species were noticeable, slightly acrid human and slightly smoky Ythrian. The latter beings were more numerous, in reversal of population figures for Avalon. But then, a number were here from elsewhere in the Domain, especially from the mother world, trying to help this frontier make ready in the crisis.

Holm forced himself to call greetings right and left as he went. His affability had become a trademark whose value he recognized. *At first it was genuine,* he thought.

The honor guard saluted and admitted him to Ferune's presence. (Holm did not tolerate time-wasting ceremoniousness in his department, but he admitted its importance to Ythrians.) The inner room was typical: spacious and sparsely furnished, a few austere decorations, bench and desk and office machinery adapted to ornithoid requirements. Rather than a transparency in the wall, there was a genuine huge window, open on garden-scented breezes and a downhill view of Gray and the waters aglitter beyond.

Ferune had added various offplanet souvenirs and a bookshelf loaded with folio copies of the Terran classics that he read, in three original languages, for enjoyment. A smallish, tan-feathered male, he was a bit of an iconoclast. His choth, Mistwood, had always been one of the most progressive on Avalon, mechanized as much as a human community and, in consequence, large and prosperous. He had scant patience to spare for tradition, religion, any conservatism. He endured a minimum of formalities because he must, but never claimed to like them.

Bouncing from his perch, he scuttled across the floor and shook hands Terran style. "Khr-r-r, good to see you, old rascal!" He spoke Planha; Ythrian throats are less versatile than human (though of course no human can ever get the sounds quite right) and he wanted neither the nuisance of wearing a vocalizer nor the grotesquerie of an accent.

"How'd it go?" Holm asked.

Ferune grimaced. But that is the wrong word. His feathers were not simply more intricate than those of Terran birds, they were more closely connected to muscles and nerve endings, and their movements constituted a whole universe of expression forever denied to man. Irritation, fret, underlying anger and dismay, rippled across his body.

"Huh." Holm found a chair designed for him, sank down, and drew tobacco pungency over his tongue. "Tell."

Foot-claws clicked on lovely-grained wood. Back and forth Ferune paced. "I'll be dictating a full report," he said. "In brief, worse than I feared. Yes, they're scrambling to establish a unified command and shove the idea of action under doctrine into every captain. But they've no dustiest notion of how to go about it."

"God on a stick," Holm exclaimed, "we've been telling them for the past five years! I thought—oh, bugger, communication's so vague in this so-called navy, I'd nothing to go on but impressions, and I guess I got the wrong ones—but you know I thought, we thought a halfway sensible reorganization was in progress."

"It was, but it moulted. Overweening pride, bickering, haggling about details. We Ythrians—our dominant culture, at least—don't fit well into anything tightly centralized." Ferune paused. "In fact," he went on, "the most influential argument against trading our separate, loosely coordinated planetary commands for a Terran-model hierarchy has been that Terra may have vastly greater forces, but these need to control a vastly greater volume of space than the Domain; and if they fight us, they'll be at the end of such a long line of communication that unified action is self-defeating."

"Huh! Hasn't it occurred to those mudbrains on Ythri, the Imperium isn't stupid? If Terra hits, it won't run the war from Terra, but from a sector close to our borders."

"We've found little sign of strength being marshaled in nearby systems."

"Certainly not!" Holm slammed a fist on the arm of his chair. "Would they give their preparations away like that? Would you? They'll assemble in space, parsecs from any star. Minimal traffic between the gathering fleet and whatever planets our scouts can sneak close to. In a few cubic light-years, they can hide power to blow us out of the plenum."

"You've told me this a few times," Ferune said dryly. "I've passed it on. To scant avail." He stopped pacing. For a while, silence dwelt in the room. The yellow light of Laura cast leaf shadows on the floor. They quivered.

"After all," Ferune said, "our methods did save us during the Troubles."

"You can't compare war lords, pirates, petty conquerors, barbarians who'd never have gotten past their stratospheres if they hadn't happened to've acquired practically self-operating ships—you can't compare that bloody-clawed rabble to Imperial Terra."

"I know," Ferune replied. "The point is, Ythrian methods served us well because they accord with Ythrian nature. I've begun to wonder, during this last trip, if an attempt to become poor copies of our rivals may not be foredoomed. The attempt's being made, understand—you'll get details till they run back out of your gorge—but could be that all we'll gain is confusion. I've decided that while Avalon must make every effort to cooperate, Avalon must at the same time expect small help from outside."

Again fell stillness. Holm looked at his superior, associate, friend of years; and not for the first time, it came to him what strangers they two were.

He found himself regarding Ferune as if he had never met an Ythrian before.

\* \* \*

Standing, the Marchwarden was about 120 centimeters high from feet to top of crest; a tall person would have gone to 140 or so, say up to the mid-breast of Holm. Since the body tilted forward, its actual length from muzzle through tail was somewhat more. It massed perhaps 20 kilos; the maximum for the species was under 30.

The head looked sculptured. It bulged back from a low brow to hold the brain. A bony ridge arched down in front to a pair of nostrils, nearly hidden by feathers, which stood above a flexible mouth full of sharp white fangs and a purple tongue. The jaw, underslung and rather delicate, merged with a strong neck. That face was dominated by its eyes, big and amber, and by the dense, scalloped feather-crest that rose from the brow, lifted over the head, and ran half the length of the neck: partly for aerodynamic purposes, partly as a helmet on the thin skull.

The torso thrust outward in a great keelbone, which at its lower end was flanked by the arms. These were not unlike the arms of a skinny human, in size and appearance; they lacked plumage, and the hide was dark yellow on Ferune's, brown or black in other Ythrian subspecies. The hands were less manlike. Each bore three fingers between two thumbs; each digit possessed one more joint than its Terran equivalent and a nail that might better be called a talon. The wrist sprouted a dew claw on its inner surface. Those hands were large in proportion to the arms, and muscles played snakishly across them; they had evolved as ripping tools, to help the teeth. The body ended in a fan-shaped tail of feathers, rigid enough to help support it when desired.

At present, though, the tremendous wings were folded down to work as legs. In the middle of either leading edge, a "knee" joint bent in reverse; those bones would lock together in flight. From the "ankle," three forward toes and one rearward extended to make a foot; aloft, they curled around the wing to strengthen and add sensitivity. The remaining three digits of the ancestral ornithoid had fused to produce the alatan bone which swept backward for more than a meter. The skin over its front half was bare, calloused, another surface to rest on.

Ferune being male, his crest rose higher than a female's, and it and the tail were white with black trim; on her they would have been of uniform dark lustrousness. The remainder of him was lighter-colored than average for his species, which ranged from gray-brown through black.

* * *

"Khr-r-r-r." The throat-noise yanked Holm out of his reverie. "You stare."

"Oh. Sorry." To a true-born carnivore, that was more rude than it was among omnivorous humans. "My mind wandered."

"Whither?" Ferune asked, mild again.

"M-m-m . . . well—well, all right. I got to thinking how little my breed really counts for in the Domain. I figure maybe we'd better assume everything's bound to be done Ythrian-style, and make the best of that."

Ferune uttered a warbling "reminder" note and quirked certain feathers. This had no exact Anglic equivalent, but the intent could be translated as: "Your sort aren't the only non-Ythrians under our hegemony. You aren't the only ones technologically up to date." Planha was in fact not as laconic as its verbal conventions made it seem.

"N-no," Holm mumbled. "But we . . . in the Empire, we're the leaders. Sure, Greater Terra includes quite a few home worlds and colonies of nonhumans; and a lot of individuals from elsewhere have gotten Terran citizenship; sure. But more humans are in key positions of every kind than members of any other race—fireflare, probably of all the other races put together." He sighed and stared at the glowing end of his cigar. "Here in the Domain, what are men? A handful on this single ball. Oh, we get around, we do well for ourselves, but the fact won't go away that we're a not terribly significant minority in a whole clutch of minorities."

"Do you regret that?" Ferune asked quite softly.

"Huh? No. No. I only meant, well, probably the Domain has too few humans to explain and administer a human-type naval organization. So better we adjust to you than you to us. It's unavoidable anyhow. Even on Avalon, where there're more of us, it's unavoidable."

"I hear a barrenness in your tone and see it in your eyes," Ferune said, more gently than was his wont. "Again you think of your son who has gone bird, true? You fear his younger brothers and sisters will fare off as he did."

Holm gathered strength to answer. "You know I respect your ways. Always have, always will. Nor am I about to forget how Ythri took my people in when Terra had rotted away beneath them. It's just . . . just . . . we rate respect too. Don't we?"

Ferune moved forward until he could lay a hand on Holm's thigh. He understood the need of humans to speak their griefs.

"When he—Chris—when he first started running around, flying around, with Ythrians, why, I was glad," the man slogged on. He held his gaze out the window. From time to time he dragged at his cigar, but the gesture was mechanical, unnoticed. "He'd always been too bookish, too alone. So his Stormgate friends, his visits there— Later, when he and Eyath and their gang were knocking around in odd corners of the planet— well, that seemed like he was doing over what I did at his age, except he'd have somebody to guard his back if a situation got sharp. I thought maybe he also would end enlisting in the navy—" Holm shook his head. "I didn't see till too late, what'd gotten in him was not old-fashioned fiddlefootedness. Then when I did wake up, and we quarreled about it, and he ran off and hid in the Shielding Islands for a year, with Eyath's help— But no point in my going on, is there?"

Ferune gestured negative. After Daniel Holm went raging to Lythran's house, accusations exploding out of him, it had been all the First Marchwarden could do to intervene, calm both parties and prevent a duel.

"No, I shouldn't have said anything today," Holm continued. "It's only—last night Rowena was crying. That he went off and didn't say goodbye to her. Mainly, she worries about what's happening to him, inside, since he joined the choth. Can he ever make a normal marriage, for instance? Ordinary girls aren't his type any more; and bird girls— And, right, our younger kids. Tommy's completely in orbit around Ythrian subjects. The school monitor had to come in person and tell us how he'd been neglecting to screen the material or submit the work or see the consultants he was supposed to. And Jeanne's found a couple of Ythrian playmates—"

"As far as I know," Ferune said, "humans who entered choths have as a rule had satisfactory lives. Problems, of course. But what life can have none? Besides, the difficulties ought to become less as the number of such persons grows."

"Look," Holm floundered, "I'm not against your folk. Break my bones if ever I was! Never once did I say or think there was anything dishonorable about what Chris was doing, any more than I would've said or thought it if, oh, if he'd joined some celibate order of priests. But I'd not have liked that either. It's no more natural for a man. And I've studied everything I could find about bird people. Sure, most of them have claimed they were happy. Probably most of them believed it. I can't help thinking they never realized what they'd missed."

"Walkers," Ferune said. In Planha, that sufficed. In Anglic he would have had to state something like: "We've lost our share, those who left the choths to become human-fashion atomic individuals within a global human community."

"Influence," he added, which conveyed: "Over the centuries on Avalon, no few of our kind have grown bitter at what your precept and example were doing to the choths themselves. Many still are. I suspect that's a major reason why several such groups have become more reactionary than any on the mother world."

Holm responded, "Wasn't the whole idea of this colony that both races should grant each other the right to be what they were?"

"That was written into the Compact and remains there," Ferune said in two syllables and three expressions. "Nobody has been compelled. But living together, how can we help changing?"

"Uh-huh. Because Ythri in general and Mistwood in particular have made a success of adopting and adapting Terran technology, you believe nothing's involved except a common-sense swap of ideas. It's not that simple, though."

"I didn't claim it is," Ferune said, "only that we don't catch time in any net."

"Yeh. I'm sorry if I— Well, I didn't mean to maunder on, especially when you've heard me often enough before. These just happen to be thin days at home." The man left his chair, strode past the Ythrian, and halted by the window, where he looked out through a veil of smoke.

"Let's get to real work," he said. "I'd like to ask specific questions about the overall state of Domain preparedness. And you'd better listen to me about what's been going on here while you were away— through the whole bloody-be-flensed Lauran System, in fact. That's none too good either."

# III

THE car identified its destination and moved down. Its initial altitude was such that the rider inside glimpsed a dozen specks of ground strewn over shining waters. But when he approached they had all fallen beneath the horizon. Only the rugged cone of St. Li was now visible to him.

* * *

With an equatorial diameter of a mere 11,308 kilometers, Avalon has a molten core smaller in proportion than Terra's; a mass of 0.635 cannot store as much heat. Thus the forces are weak that thrust land upward. At the same time, erosion proceeds fast. The atmospheric pressure at sea level is similar to the Terrestrial—and drops off more slowly with height, because of the gravity gradient—and rapid rotation

makes for violent weather. In consequence, the surface is generally low, the highest peak in the Andromedas rising no more than 4500 meters. Nor does the
land occur in great masses. Corona, capping the north
pole and extending down past the Tropic of Swords,
covers barely eight million square kilometers, about
the size of Australia. In the opposite hemisphere,
Equatoria, New Africa, and New Gaiila could better
be called large islands than minor continents. All else
consists of far smaller islands.

Yet one feature is gigantic. Some 2000 kilometers
due west of Gray begins that drowned range whose
peaks, thrusting into air, are known as Oronesia.
Southward it runs, crosses the Tropic of Spears, trails
off at last not far from the Antarctic Circle. Thus it
forms a true, hydrological boundary; its western side
marks off the Middle Ocean, its eastern the Hesperian
Sea in the northern hemisphere and the South Ocean
beyond the equator. It supports a distinct ecology,
incredibly rich. And thereby, after the colonization, it
became a sociological phenomenon. Any eccentrics,
human or Ythrian, could go off, readily transform one
or a few isles, and make their own undisturbed
existence.

The mainland choths were diverse in size as well
as in organization and tradition. But whether they be
roughly analogous to clans, tribes, baronies, religious
communes, republics, or whatever, they counted their
members in the thousands at least. In Oronesia there
were single households which bore the name; grown
and married, the younger children were expected to
found new, independent societies.

Naturally, this extremism was exceptional. The
Highsky folk in particular were numerous, controlling
the fisheries around latitude 30° N. and occupying
quite a stretch of the archipelago. And they were fairly
conventional, insofar as that word has any meaning
when applied to Ythrians.

* * *

The aircar landed on the beach below a compound. He who stepped out was tall, with dark-red hair, clad in sandals, kilt, and weapons.

Tabitha Falkayn had seen the vehicle descending and walked forth to meet it. "Hello, Christopher Holm," she said in Anglic.

"I come as Arinnian," he answered in Planha. "Luck fare beside you, Hrill."

She smiled. "Excuse me if I don't elaborate the occasion." Shrewdly: "You called ahead that you wanted to see me on a public matter. That must have to do with the border crisis. I daresay your Khruath decided that western Corona and northern Oronesia must work out a means of defending the Hesperian Sea."

He nodded awkwardly, and his eyes sought refuge from her amusement.

Enormous overhead, sunshine brilliant off cumulus banks, arched heaven. A sailor winged yonder, scouting for schools of piscoid; a flock of Ythrian shuas flapped by under the control of a herder and his uhoths; native pteropleuron lumbered around a reef rookery. The sea rolled indigo, curled in translucent green breakers, and exploded in foam on sands nearly as white. Trawlers plied it, kilometers out. Inland the ground rose steep. The upper slopes still bore a pale emerald mat of susin; only a few kinds of shrub were able to grow past those interlocking roots. But further down the hills had been plowed. There Ythrian clustergrain rustled red, for ground cover and to feed the shuas, while groves of coconut palm, mango, orange, and pumpernickel plant lifted above to nourish the human members of Highsky. A wind blew, warm but fresh, full of salt and iodine and fragrances.

"I suppose it was felt bird-to-bird conferences would be a good idea," Tabitha went on. "You mountaineers will have ample trouble understanding us

pelagics, and vice versa, without the handicap of dif-
fering species. Ornithoids will meet likewise, hm?"
Her manner turned thoughtful: "You had to be a dele-
gate, of course. Your area has so few of your kind.
But why come in person? Not that you aren't welcome. Still, a phone call—"

"We . . . we may have to talk at length," he said.
"For days, off and on." He took for granted he would
receive hospitality; all choths held that a guest was
sacred.

"Why me, though? I'm only a local."

"You're a descendant of David Falkayn."

"That doesn't mean much."

"It does where I live. Besides—well, we've met
before, now and then, at the larger Khruaths and on
visits to each other's home areas and—We're acquainted
a little. I'd not know where to begin among total
strangers. If nothing else, you . . . you can advise me
whom to consult, and introduce me. Can't you?"

"Certainly." Tabitha took both his hands. "Besides, I'm
glad to see you, Chris."

His heart knocked. He struggled not to squirm.
*What makes me this shy before her?* God knew she
was attractive. A few years older than he, big, strongly
built, full-breasted and long of leg, she showed to
advantage in a short sleeveless tunic. Her face was
snubnosed, wide of mouth, its green eyes set far apart
under heavy brows; she had never bothered to remove
the white scar on her right cheekbone. Her hair,
cropped beneath the ears, was bleached flaxen. It blew
like banners over the brown, slightly freckled skin.

He wondered if she went as casually to bed as the
Coronan bird girls—never with a male counterpart;
always a hearty, husky, not overintelligent worker
type—or if she was a virgin. That seemed unlikely.
What human, perpetually in a low-grade lovetime,
could match the purity of an Eyath? Yet Highsky
wasn't Stormgate or The Tarns—he didn't know—

Tabitha had no companions of her own species here where she dwelt—however, she traveled often and widely. . . . He cast the speculation from him.

"Hoy, you're blushing," she laughed. "Did I violate one of your precious mores?" She released him. "If so, I apologize. But you always take these things too seriously. Relax. A social rite or a social gaffe isn't a deathpride matter."

*Easy for her, I suppose,* he thought. *Her grandparents were received into this choth. Her parents and their children grew up in it. A fourth of the membership must be human by now. And they've influenced it—like this commercial fishery she and Draun have started, a strictly private enterprise—*

"I'm afraid we've no time for gaiety," he got out. "We've walking weather ahead."

"Indeed?"

"The Empire's about to expand our way."

"C'mon to the house." Tabitha took his arm and urged him toward the compound. Its thatch-roofed timber dwellings were built lower than most Ythrian homes and were sturdier than they seemed; for here was scant protection from Avalon's hurricanes. "Oh, yes," she said, "the empire's been growing vigorously since Manuel the First. But I've read its history. How has the territory been brought under control? Some by simple partnership—civilized nonhumans like the Cynthians found it advantageous. Some by purchase or exchange. Some by conquest, yes—but always of primitives, or at most of people whose strength in space was ridiculously less than Greater Terra's. We're a harder gale to buck."

"Are we? My father says—"

"Uh-huh. The Empire's sphere approaches 400 light-years across, ours about 80. Out of all the systems in its volume, the Empire's got a degree of direct contact with several thousand, we with barely 250. But don't you see, Chris, we know our planets better?

We're more compact. Our total resources are less but our technology's every bit as good. And then, we're distant from Terra. Why should they attack us? We don't threaten them, we merely claim our rights along the border. If they want more realm, they can find plenty closer to home, suns they've never visited, and easier to acquire than from a proud, well-armed Domain."

"My father says we're weak and unready."

"Do you think we would lose a war?"

He fell silent until they both noticed, through the soughing ahead, how sand scrunched beneath their feet. At last: "Well, I don't imagine anybody goes into a war expecting to lose."

"I don't believe they'll fight," Tabitha said. "I believe the Imperium has better sense."

"Regardless, we'd better take precautions. Home defense is among them."

"Yes. Won't be easy to organize, among a hundred or more sovereign choths."

"That's where we birds come in, maybe," he ventured. "Long established ones in particular, like your family."

"I'm honored to help," she told him. "And in fact I don't imagine the choths will cooperate too badly—" she tossed her head in haughtiness—"when it's a matter of showing the Empire who flies highest!"

Eyath and Vodan winged together. They made a handsome pair, both golden of eyes and arms, he ocher-brown and she deep bronze. Beneath them reached the Stormgate lands, forest-darkened valleys, crags and cliffs, peaks where snowfields lingered to dapple blue-gray rock, swordblade of a waterfall and remote blink of a glacier. A wind sang *whoo* and drove clouds, which Laura tinged gold, through otherwise brilliant air; their shadows raced and rippled across the world. The Ythrians drank of the wind's cold and swam in its swirling, thrusting, flowing strength. It stroked their feathers till they felt the barbs of the great outer pinions shiver.

He said: "If we were of Arinnian's kind, I would surely wed you, now, before I go to my ship. But you won't be in lovetime for months, and by then I might be dead. I would not bind you to that sorrow for nothing."

"Do you think I would grieve less if I had not the name of widow?" she answered. "I'd want the right to lead your memorial dance. For I know what parts of these skies you like best."

"Still, you would have to lift some awkward questions, obligation toward my blood and so on. No. Shall our friendship be less because, for a while, you have not the name of wife?"

"Friendship—" she murmured. Impulsively: "I dreamt last night that we were indeed like humans."

"What, forever in rut?"

"Forever in love."

"Kh-h'ng, I've naught against Arinnian, but sometimes I wonder if you've not been too much with him, for too many years since you both were small. Had Lythran not taken you along when he had business in Gray—" Vodan saw her crest rise, broke off and added in haste: "Yes, he's your galemate. That makes him mine too. I only wanted to warn you . . . don't try, don't wish to be human."

"No, no." Eyath felt a downdraft slide by. She slanted herself to catch it, a throb of wings and then the long wild glide, peaks leaping nearer, glimpse through trees of a pool ashine where a feral stallion drank, song and rush and caress of cloven air, till she checked herself and flew back upward, breasting a torrent, every muscle at full aliveness—traced a thermal by the tiny trembling of a mountain seen through it, won there, spread her wings and let heaven carry her hovering while she laughed.

Vodan beat near. "Would I trade this?" she called joyously. "Or you?"

Ekrem Saracoglu, Imperial governor of Sector Pacis, had hinted for a while that he would like to meet the daughter of Fleet Admiral Juan de Jesús Cajal y Palomares. She had come from Nuevo México to be official hostess and feminine majordomo for her widowed father, after he transferred his headquarters to Esperance and rented a house in Fleurville. The date kept being postponed. It was not that the admiral disliked the governor—they got along well—nor distrusted his intentions, no matter how notorious a womanizer he was. Luisa had been raised among folk who, if strict out of necessity on their dry world, were rich in honor and bore a hair-trigger pride. It was merely that both men were overwhelmed by work.

At last their undertakings seemed fairly well along, and Cajal invited Sarocoglu to dinner. A ridiculous last-minute contretemps occurred. The admiral phoned home that he would be detained at the office a couple of hours. The governor was already on his way.

"Thus you, Donna, have been told to keep me happy in the teeth of a postponed meal," Saracoglu purred over the hand he kissed. "I assure you, that will not be in the least difficult." Though small, she had a lively figure and a darkly pretty face. And he soon learned that, albeit solemn, she knew how to listen to a man and, rarer yet, ask him stimulating questions.

By then they were strolling in the garden. Rose-bushes and cherry trees might almost have been growing on Terra; Esperance was a prize among colony planets. The sun Pax was still above the horizon, now at midsummer, but leveled mellow beams across an old brick wall. The air was warm, blithe with birdsong, sweet with green odors that drifted in from the countryside. A car or two caught the light, high above; but

Fleurville was not big enough for its traffic noise to be heard this far from the centrum.

Saracoglu and Luisa paced along graveled paths and talked. They were guarded, which is to say discreetly chaperoned. However, no duenna followed several paces behind, but a huge four-armed Gorzunian mercenary on whom the nuances of a flirtation would be lost.

*The trouble is,* thought the governor, *she's begun conversing in earnest.*

It had been quite pleasant at first. She encouraged him to speak of himself. "—yes, the Earl of Anatolia, that's me. Frankly, even if it is on Terra, a minor peerage. . . . Career bureaucrat. Might rather've been an artist—I dabble in oils and clays—maybe you'd care to see. . . . Alas, you know how such things go. Imperial nobles are expected to serve the Imperium. Had I but been born in a decadent era! Eh? Unfortunately, the Empire's not run out of momentum—"

Inwardly, he grinned at his own performance. He, fifty-three standard years of age, squat, running to fat, totally bald, little eyes set close to a giant nose, and two expensive mistresses in his palace—acting the role of a boy who acted the role of an *homme du monde!* Well, he enjoyed that once in a while, as he enjoyed gaudy clothes and jewels. They were a relaxation from the wry realism which had never allowed him to improve his appearance through biosculp.

But at this point she asked, "Are we really going to attack the Ythrians?"

"Heh?" The distress in her tone brought his head swinging sharply around to stare at her. "Why, negotiations are stalled, but—"

"Who stalled them?" She kept her own gaze straight ahead. Her voice had risen a note and the slight Espanyol accent had intensified.

"Who started most of the violent incidents?" he countered. "Ythrians. Not that they're monsters, understand. But they are predators by nature. And they've no strong authority—no proper government at all—to control the impulses of groups. That's been a major stumbling block in the effort to reach an accommodation."

"How genuine was the effort—on our side?" she demanded, still refusing to look at him. "How long have you planned to fall on them? My father won't tell me anything, but it's obvious, it's been obvious ever since he moved here—how often are naval and civilian headquarters on the same planet?—it's obvious something is b-b-being readied."

"Donna," Saracoglu said gravely, "when a fleet of spacecraft can turn whole worlds into tombs, one prepares against the worst and one clamps down security regulations." He paused. "One also discovers it is unwise to let spheres interpenetrate, as Empire and Domain have. I daresay you, young, away off in a relatively isolated system . . . I daresay you got an idea the Imperium is provoking war in order to swallow the whole Ythrian Domain. That is not true."

"What is true?" she replied bitterly.

"That there have been bloody clashes over disputed territories and conflicting interests."

"Yes. Our traders are losing potential profits."

"Would that were the only friction. Commercial disputes are always negotiable. Political and military rivalries are harder. For example, which of us shall absorb the Antoranite-Kraokan complex around Beta Centauri? One of us is bound to, and those resources would greatly strengthen Terra. The Ythrians have already gained more power, by bringing Dathyna under them, than we like a potentially hostile race to have.

"Furthermore, by rectifying this messy frontier, we can armor ourselves against a Merseian flank attack." Saracoglu lifted a hand to forestall her protest. "Indeed, Donna, the Roidhunate is far off and not very big. But it's growing at an alarming rate, and aggressive acquisitiveness is built into its ideology. The duty of an empire is to provide for the great-grandchildren."

"Why can't we simply write a treaty, give a *quid pro quo,* divide things in a fair and reasonable manner?" Luisa asked.

Saracoglu sighed. "The populations of the planets would object to being treated like inanimate property. No government which took that attitude would long survive." He gestured aloft. "Furthermore, the universe holds too many unknowns. We have traveled hundreds—in earlier days, thousands—of light-years to especially interesting stars. But what myriads have we bypassed? What may turn up when we do seek them out? No responsible authority, human or Ythrian, will blindly hand over such possibilities to an alien.

"No, Donna, this is no problem capable of neat, final solutions. We just have to do our fumbling best. Which does *not* include subjugating Ythri. I'm the first to grant Ythri's right to exist, go its own way, even keep offplanet possessions. But this frontier must be stabilized."

"We—interpenetrate—with others—and have no trouble."

"Of course. Why should we fight hydrogen breathers, for example? They're so exotic we can barely communicate with them. The trouble is, the Ythrians are too like us. As an old, old saying goes, two tough, smart races want the same real estate."

"We can live with them! Humans are doing it. They have for generations."

"Do you mean Avalon?"

She nodded.

Saracoglu saw a chance to divert the conversation back into easier channels. "Well, there's an interesting case, certainly," he smiled. "How much do you know about it?"

"Very little," she admitted, subdued. "A few mentions here and there, since I came to Esperance. The galaxy's so huge, this tiny fleck of it we've explored. . . ."

"You might get to see Avalon," he said. "Not far off, ten or twelve light-years. I'd like that myself. The society does appear to be unusual, if not absolutely unique."

"Don't you understand? If humans and Ythrians can share a single planet—"

"That's different. Allow me to give you some background. I've never been there either, but I've studied material on it since getting this appointment."

Saracoglu drew breath. "Avalon was discovered five hundred years ago, by the same Grand Survey ship that came on Ythri," he said. "It was noted as a potential colony, but was so remote from Terra that nobody was interested then; the very name wasn't bestowed till long afterward. Ythri was forty light-years further, true, but much more attractive, a rich planet full of people vigorously entering the modern era who had a considerable deal to trade.

"About three and a half centuries back, a human company made the Ythrians a proposal. The Polesotechnic League wasn't going to collapse for another fifty years, but already anybody who had a functional brain could read what a cutthroat period lay ahead. These humans, a mixed lot under the leadership of an old trade pioneer, wanted to safeguard the future of their families by settling on out-of-the-way Avalon— under the suzerainty, the protection, of an Ythri that was not corrupted as Technic civilization was. The Ythrians agreed, and naturally some of them joined the settlement.

"Well, the Troubles came, and Ythri was not spared. The eventual results were similar—Terra enforced peace by the Empire, Ythri by the Domain. In the meantime, standing together, bearing the brunt of chaos, the Avalonians had been welded into one.

"Nothing like that applies today."

They had stopped by a vine-covered trellis. He plucked a grape and offered it to her. She shook her head. He ate it himself. The taste held a slight, sweet strangeness; Esperancian soil was not, after all, identical with that of Home. The sun was now gone from sight, shadows welled in the garden, an evening star blossomed.

"I suppose ... your plans for 'rectification' ... include bringing Avalon into the Empire," Luisa said.

"Yes. Consider its position." Saracoglu shrugged. "Besides, the humans there form a large majority. I rather imagine they'll be glad to join us, and Ythri won't mind getting rid of them."

"Must we fight?"

Saracoglu smiled. "It's never too late for peace." He took her arm. "Shall we go indoors? I expect your father will be here soon. We ought to have the sherry set out for him."

He'd not spoil the occasion, which was still salvageable, by telling her that weeks had passed since a courier ship brought what he requested: an Imperial rescript declaring war on Ythri, to be made public whenever governor and admiral felt ready to act.

# IV

A campaign against Ythri would demand an enormous fleet, gathered from everywhere in the Empire. No such thing had been publicly seen or heard of, though rumors flew. But of course units guarding the border systems had been openly reinforced as the crisis sharpened, and drills and practice maneuvers went on apace.

Orbiting Pax at ten astronomical units, the Planet-class cruisers *Thor* and *Ansa* flung blank shells and torpedoes at each other's force screens, pierced these latter with laser beams that tried to hold on a single spot of hull for as long as an energy blast would have taken to gnaw through armor, exploded magnesium flares whose brilliance represented lethal radiation, dodged about on grav thrust, wove in and out of

41

hyperdrive phase, used every trick in the book and a few which the high command hoped had not yet gotten into Ythrian books. Meanwhile the Comet- and Meteor-class boats they mothered were similarly busy.

To stimulate effort, a prize had been announced. That vessel the computers judged victorious would proceed with her auxiliaries to Esperance, where the crew would get a week's liberty.

*Ansa* won. She broadcast a jubilant recall. Half a million kilometers away, an engine awoke in the Meteor which her captain had dubbed *Hooting Star*.

"Resurrected at last!" Lieutenant (j.g.) Philippe Rochefort exulted. "And in glory at that."

"And unearned." The fire control officer, CPO Wa Chaou of Cynthia, grinned. His small white-furred body crouched on the table he had been cleaning after a meal; his bushy tail quivered like the whiskers around his blue-masked muzzle.

"What the muck you mean, 'unearned'?" the engineer-computerman, CPO Abdullah Helu, grumbled: a lean, middle-aged careerist from Huy Braseal. "Playing dead for three mortal days is beyond the call of duty." The boat had theoretically been destroyed in a dogfight and drifting free, as a real wreck would, to complicate life for detector technicians.

"Especially when the poker game cleaned and reamed you, eh?" Wa Chaou gibed.

"I won't play with you again, sir," Helu said to the captain-pilot. "No offense. You're just too mucking talented."

"Only luck," Rochefort answered. "Same as it was only luck that threw such odds against us. The boat acquitted herself well. As you did afterward, over the chips. Better luck to both next time."

She was his first, new and shiny command—he having recently been promoted from ensign for audacity in a rescue operation—and he was anxious for her to make a good showing. No matter how inevitable under the circumstances, defeat had hurt.

But they were on the top team; and they'd accounted for two opposition craft, plus tying up three more for a while that must have been used to advantage elsewhere; and now they were bound back to *Ansa* and thence to Esperance, where he knew enough girls that dates were a statistical certainty.

The little cabin trembled and hummed with driving energies. Air gusted from ventilators, smelling of oil and of recycling chemicals. A Meteor was designed for high acceleration under both relativistic and hyperdrive conditions; for accurate placement of nuclear-headed torpedoes; and for no more comfort than minimally essential to the continued efficiency of personnel.

Yet space lay around the viewports in a glory of stars, diamond-keen, unwinking, many-colored, crowding an infinitely clear blackness till they merged in the argent torrent of the Milky Way or the dim mysterious cloudlets which were sister galaxies. Rochefort wanted to sit, look, let soul follow gaze outward into God's temple the universe. He could have done so, too; the boat was running on full automatic. But better demonstrate to the others that he was a conscientious as well as an easy-going officer. He turned the viewer back on which he had been using when the message came.

A canned lecture was barely under way. A human xenologist stood in the screen and intoned:

"Warm-blooded, feathered, and flying, the Ythrians are not birds; they bring their young forth viviparously after a gestation of four and a half months; they do not have beaks, but lips and teeth. Nor are they mammals; they grow no hair and secrete no milk; those lips have developed for parents to feed infants by regurgitation. And while the antlibranchs might suggest fish gills, they are not meant for water but for—"

"Oh, no!" Helu exclaimed. "Sir, won't you have

time to study later? Devil knows how many more weeks we'll lie in orbit doing nothing."

"War may erupt at any minute," Wa Chaou said.

"And if and when, who cares how the enemy looks or what his love life is? His ships are about like ours, and that's all we're ever likely to see."

"Oh, you have a direct line to the future?" the Cynthian murmured.

Rochefort stopped the tape and snapped, "I'll put the sound on tight beam if you want. But a knowledge of the enemy's nature might make the quantum of difference that saves us when the real thing happens. I suggest you watch too."

"Er, I think I should check out Number Three oscillator, long's we're not traveling faster-than-light," Helu said, and withdrew into the engine room. Wa Chaou settled down by Rochefort.

The lieutenant smiled. He refrained from telling the Cynthian, *You're a good little chap. Did you enlist to get away from the domination of irascible females on your home planet?*

His thought went on: *The reproductive pattern—sexual characteristics, requirements of the young—does seem to determine most of the basics in any intelligent species. As if the cynic's remark were true, that an organism is simply a DNA molecule's way of making more DNA molecules. Or whatever the chemicals of heredity may be on a given world. . . . But no, a Jerusalem Catholic can't believe that. Biological evolution inclines, it does not compel.*

"Let's see how the Ythrians work," he said aloud, reaching for the switch.

"Don't you already know, sir?" Wa Chaou asked.

"Not really. So many sophont races, in that bit of space we've sort of explored. And I've been busy familiarizing myself with my new duties." Rochefort chuckled. "And, be it admitted, enjoying what leaves I could get."

He reactivated the screen. It showed an Ythrian walking on the feet that grew from his wings: a comparatively slow, jerky gait, no good for real distances. The being stopped, lowered hands to ground, and stood on them. He lifted his wings, and suddenly he was splendid.

Beneath, on either side, were slits in column. As the wings rose, the feathery operculum-like flaps which protected them were drawn back. The slits widened until, at full extension, they gaped like purple mouths. The view became a closeup. Thin-skinned tissues, intricately wrinkled, lay behind a curtain of cilia which must be for screening out dust.

When the wings lowered, the slits were forced shut again, bellows fashion. The lecturer's voice said: "This is what allows so heavy a body, under Terra-type weight and gas density, to fly. Ythrians attain more than twice the mass of the largest possible airborne creature on similar planets elsewhere. The antlibranchs, pumped by the wingstrokes, take in oxygen under pressure to feed it directly to the bloodstream. Thus they supplement lungs which themselves more or less resemble those of ordinary land animals. The Ythrian acquires the power needed to get aloft and, indeed, fly with rapidity and grace."

The view drew back. The creature in the holograph flapped strongly and rocketed upward.

"Of course," the dry voice said, "this energy must come from a correspondingly accelerated metabolism. Unless prevented from flying, the Ythrian is a voracious eater. Aside from certain sweet fruits, he is strictly carnivorous. His appetite has doubtless reinforced the usual carnivore tendency to live in small, well-separated groups, each occupying a wide territory which instinct makes it defend against all intruders.

"In fact, the Ythrian can best be understood in terms of what we know or conjecture about the evolution of his race."

"Conjecture more than know, I suspect," Rochefort remarked. But he found himself fascinated.

\* \* \*

"We believe that homeothermic—roughly speaking, warm-blooded—life on Ythri did not come from a reptilian or reptiloid form, but directly from an amphibian, conceivably even from something corresponding to a lungfish. At any rate, it retained a kind of gill. Those species which were most successful on land eventually lost this feature. More primitive animals kept it. Among these was that small, probably swamp-dwelling thing which became the ancestor of the sophont. Taking to the treetops, it may have developed a membrane on which to glide from bough to bough. This finally turned into a wing. Meanwhile the gills were modified for aerial use, into superchargers."

"As usual," Wa Chaou observed. "The failures at one stage beget the successes of the next."

"Of course, the Ythrian can soar and even hover," the speaker said, "but it is the tremendous wing area which makes this possible, and the antlibranchs are what make it possible to operate those wings.

"Otherwise the pre-Ythrian must have appeared fairly similar to Terran birds." Pictures of various hypothetical extinct creatures went by. "It developed an analogous water-hoarding system—no separate urination—which saved weight as well as compensating for evaporative losses from the antlibranchs. It likewise developed light bones, though these are more intricate than avian bones, built of a marvelously strong two-phase material whose organic component is not collagen but a substance carrying out the functions of Terra-mammalian marrow. The animal did not, however, further ease its burdens by trading teeth for a beak. Many Ythrian ornithoids have done so, for example the uhoth, hawklike in appearance, doglike in service. But the pre-sophont remained an unspecialized dweller in wet jungles.

"The fact that the young were born tiny and help-less—since the female could not fly long distances while carrying a heavy fetus—is probably responsible for the retention and elaboration of the digits on the wings. The cub could cling to either parent in turn while these cruised after food; before it was able to fly, it could save itself from enemies by clambering up a tree. Meanwhile the feet acquired more and more ability to seize prey and manipulate objects.

"Incidentally, the short gestation period does not mean that the Ythrian is born with a poorly developed nervous system. The rapid metabolism of flight affects the rate of fetal cell division. This process concentrates on laying down a body pattern rather than on increasing the size. Nevertheless, an infant Ythrian needs more care, and more food, than an infant human. The parents must cooperate in providing this as well as in carrying their young about. Here we may have the root cause of the sexual equality or near equality found in all Ythrian cultures.

"Likewise, a rapid succession of infants would be impossible to keep alive under primitive conditions. This may be a reason why the female only ovulates at intervals of a year—Ythri's is about half of Terra's—and not for about two years after giving birth. Sexuality does not come overtly into play except at these times. Then it is almost uncontrollably strong in male and female alike. This may well have given the territorial instinct a cultural reinforcement after intelligence evolved. Parents wish to keep their nubile daughters isolated from chance-met males while in heat. Furthermore, husband and wife do not wish to waste a rich, rare experience on any outsider.

"The sexual cycle is not totally rigid. In particular, grief often brings on estrus. Doubtless this was originally a provision of nature for rapid replacement of losses. It seems to have brought about a partial fusion of Eros and Thanatos in the Ythrian psyche which makes much of the race's art, and doubtless thought, incomprehensible to man. An occasional female can ovulate at will, though this is considered an abnormality; in olden days she would be killed, now she is generally shunned, out of dread of her power. A favorite villain in Ythrian story is the male who, by hypnosis or otherwise, can induce the state. Of course, the most important manifestation of a degree of flexibility is the fact that Ythrians have successfully adapted their reproductive pattern, like everything else, to a variety of colonized planets."

"Me, I think it's more fun being human," Rochefort said.

"I don't know, sir," Wa Chaou replied. "Superficially the relationship between the sexes looks simpler than in your race or mine; you're either in the mood or you're not, and that's that. I wonder, though, if it may not really be more subtle and complicated than ours, even more basic to the whole psychology."

"But to return to evolution," the lecturer was saying. "It seems that a major part of Ythri underwent something like the great Pliocene drought in Terra's Africa. The ornithoids were forced out of dwindling forests onto growing savannahs. There they evolved from carrion eaters to big-game hunters in a manner analogous to pre-man. The original feet became hands, which eventually started making tools. To support the body and provide locomotion on the ground, the original elbow claws turned into feet, the wings that bore them became convertible to legs of a sort.

"Still, the intelligent Ythrian remained a pure carnivore, and one which was awkward on land. Typically, primitive hunters struck from above, with spears, arrows, axes. Thus only a few were needed to bring down the largest beasts. There was no necessity to cooperate in digging pits for elephants or standing shoulder to shoulder against a charging lion. Society remained divided into families or clans, which seldom fought wars but which, on the other hand, did not have much contact of any sort.

"The revolution which ended the Stone Age did not involve agriculture from the beginning, as in the case of man. It came from the systematic herding, at last the domestication, of big ground animals like the maukh, smaller ones like the long-haired mayaw. This stimulated the invention of skids, wheels, and the like, enabling the Ythrian to get about more readily on the surface. Agriculture was invented as an ancillary to ranching, an efficient means of providing fodder. The food surplus allowed leisure for travel, trade, and widespread cultural intercourse. Hence larger, complex social units arose.

"They cannot be called civilizations in a strict sense, because Ythri has never known true cities. The mobility of being winged left no necessity for crowding together in order to maintain close relationships. Granted, sedentary centers did appear—for mining, metallurgy, and other industry; for trade and religion; for defense in case the group was defeated by another in aerial battle. But these have always been small and their populations mostly floating. Apart from their barons and garrisons, their permanent inhabitants were formerly, for the main part, wing-clipped slaves— today, automated machines. Clipping was an easy method of making a person controllable; yet since the feathers could grow back, the common practice of promising manumission after a certain period of diligent service tended to make prisoners docile. Hence slavery became so basic to pre-industrial Ythrian society that to this day it has not entirely disappeared."

*Well, we're reviving it in the Empire,* Rochefort thought. *For terms and under conditions limited by law; as a punishment, in order to get some social utility out of the criminal; nevertheless, we're bringing back a thing the Ythrians are letting die. How more moral are we than they? How much more right do we have?*

He straightened in his chair. *Man is my race.*

\* \* \*

A willowy blonde with the old-fashioned Esperancian taste for simplicity in clothes, Eve Davisson made a pleasing contrast to Philippe Rochefort, as both were well aware. He was a tall, rather slender young man, his bearing athletic, his features broadnosed, full-lipped, and regular, his hair kinking itself into a lustrous black coif over the deep-brown skin. And he stretched to the limit the tolerance granted officers as regards their dress uniforms—rakishly tilted bonnet bearing the sunburst of Empire, gold-trimmed blue tunic, scarlet sash and cloak, snowy trousers tucked into low boots of authentic Terran beef-leather.

They sat in an intimate restaurant of Fleurville, by a window opening on gardens and stars. A live sonorist played something old and sentimental; perfumed, slightly intoxicant vapors drifted about; they toyed with hors d'oeuvres and paid more serious attention to their champagne. Nonetheless she was not smiling.

"This world was settled by people who believed in peace," she said. Her tone mourned rather than accused. "For generations they kept no armed forces, they relied on the good will of others whom they helped."

"That good will didn't outlive the Troubles," Rochefort said.

"I know, I know. I shan't join the demonstrators, whatever some of my friends may say when they learn I've been out with an Imperial officer. But Phil—the star named Pax, the planet named Esperance are being geared for war. It hurts."

"It'd hurt worse if you were attacked. Avalon isn't far, and they've built a lot of power there."

Her fingers tightened on the stem of her glass. "Attack from Avalon? But I've *met* those people, both races. They've come here on trade or tour or—I made a tour there myself, not long ago. I went because it's picturesque, but was so graciously treated I didn't want to leave."

"I daresay Ythrian manners have rubbed off on their human fellows." Rochefort let a draft go over his palate, hoping it would tingle away his irritation. This wasn't supposed to be a political evening. "Likewise less pleasant features of the Ythrian personality."

She studied him through the soft light before she said low, "I get an impression you disapprove of a mixed colony."

"Well . . . in a way, yes." He could have dissembled, facilely agreed to everything she maintained, and thus improved his chances of bedding her later on. But he'd never operated thus; and he never would, especially when he liked this girl just as a person. "I believe in being what you are and standing by your own."

"You talk almost like a human supremacist," she said, though mildly.

"To the extent that man is the leading race—furnishes most of the leaders—in Technic civilization, yes, I suppose you'd have to call me a human supremacist," he admitted. "It doesn't mean we aren't chronically sinful and stupid, nor does it mean we have any right to oppress others. Why, my sort of people are the xenosophont's best friend. We simply don't want to imitate him."

"Do you believe the Terran Empire is a force for good?"

"On balance, yes. It commits evil. But nothing mortal can avoid that. Our duty is to correct the wrongs . . . and also to recognize the values that the Empire does, in fact, preserve."

"You may have encountered too little of the evil."

"Because I'm from Terra itself?" Rochefort chuckled. "My dear, you're too bright to imagine the mother system is inhabited exclusively by aristocrats. My father is a minor functionary in the Sociodynamic Service. His job caused us to move around a lot. I was born in Selenopolis, which is a spaceport and manufacturing center. I spent several impressionable years on Venus, in the crime and poverty of a planet whose terraforming never had been quite satisfactory. I joined the navy as an enlisted rating—not out of chauvinism, merely a boyish wish to see the universe— and wasn't tapped for pilot school for two-three years; meanwhile, I saw the grim side of more than one world. Sure, there's a cosmos of room for improvement. Well, let's improve, not tear down. And let's defend!"

He stopped. "Damn," he said frankly. "I'd hoped to lure you out of your seriousness, and fell into it myself."

Now the girl laughed, and raised her glass. "Let's help each other climb out, then," she suggested.

They did. Rochefort's liberty became highly enjoyable. And that was fortunate, because two weeks after he reported back from it, *Ansa* was ordered into deep space. Light-years from Pax, she joined the fleet that had been using immensity as a mask for its marshaling; and ships by the hundreds hurled toward the Domain of Ythri.

# V

THE conference was by phone. Most were, these days. It went against old Avalonian courtliness but saved time—and time was getting in mighty short supply, Daniel Holm thought.

Anger crackled through clearly enough. Two of the three holographs on the com board before him seemed about to climb out of their screens and into his office. No doubt he gave their originals the same impression.

Matthew Vickery, President of the Parliament of Man, wagged his forefinger and both plump jowls and said, "We are not under a military regime, may I remind you in case you have forgotten. We, the proper civil government, approved your defense measures of the past several years, though you are aware that I

myself have always considered them excessive. When
I think of the prosperity that tax money, those
resources, could have brought, left in private hands—
or the social good it could have done in the public
sector— Give you military your heads, and you'd build
bases in the fourth dimension to protect us against an
invasion from the future."

"We are always being invaded by the future," Ferune said. "The next part of it to arrive will not be
pleasant."

Holm crossed his legs, leaned back, blew cigar
smoke at Vickery's image, and drawled, "Spare us the
oratory. You're not campaigning for re-election here.
What's made you demand this four-way?"

"Your entire high-handedness," Vickery declared.
"The overflow quantum was that last order, barring
non-Ythrian ships from the Lauran System. Do you
realize what a trade we do ... not merely with the
Empire, though that supports many livelihoods, but
with unaffiliated civilizations like the Kraokan?"

"Do *you* realize how easy it'd be for the Terrans
to get a robotic job, disguised, into low orbit around
Avalon?" Holm retorted. "Several thousand megatons,
touched off at that height when skies are clear, would
set about half of Corona afire. Or it might be so
sophisticated it could land like a peaceful mer-
chantman. Consciousness-level computers aren't used
much any more, when little new exploration's going
on, but they could be built, including a suicide imper-
ative. That explosion would be inside a city's force
shields; it'd take out the generators, leaving what was
left of the city defenseless; fallout from a dirty warhead would poison the whole hinterland. And you,
Vickery, helped block half the appropriation we
wanted for adequate shelters."

"Hysteria," the president said. "What could Terra
gain from a one-shot atrocity? Not that I expect war,
if only we can curb our own hotheads. But—well, take

this ludicrous home-guard program you've instigated."
His glance went toward Ferune and Liaw. "Oh, it
gives a lot of young folk a fine excuse to swagger
around, getting in people's way, ordering them arro-
gantly about, feeling important, and never mind the
social as well as the fiscal cost of it. But if this navy
we've been building and manning at your loud urging,
by straining our production facilities and gutting our
resources, if this navy is as advertised, the Terrans
can never come near us. If not, who has been derelict
in his duty?"

"We are near their sector capital," Ferune reminded
him. "They may strike us first, overwhelmingly."

"I've heard that till I'm taped for it. I prefer to
program myself, thank you." Vickery paused. "See
here," he continued in a leveled tone, "I agree the
situation is critical. We're all Avalonians together. If I
feel certain of your proposals are unwise, I tell this to
the public and the Parliament. But in the end we
compromise like reasonable beings."

Ferune's face rippled. It was as well that Vickery
didn't notice or wasn't able to read the meaning. Liaw
of The Tarns remained expressionless. Holm grunted.
"Go on."

"I must protest both your proceedings and the manner of them," Vickery said. "We are not under martial
law, and indeed the Compact makes no provision for
declaring it."

"Wasn't needed in the old days," Holm said. "The
danger was clear and present. I didn't think it'd be
needed now. The Admiralty is responsible for local
defense and liaison with armed forces elsewhere in
the Domain—"

"Which does *not* authorize you to stop trade, or
raise a tin militia, or anything cutting that deeply into
normal Avalonian life. My colleagues and I have
endured it thus far, recognizing the necessity of at
least some things. But today the necessity is to remind

you that you are the servants of the people, not the masters. If the people want your policies executed, they will so instruct their legislative representatives."

"The Khruaths did call for a home guard and for giving the Admiralty broad discretion," Liaw of The Tarns said in his rustling voice. He was old, had frost in his feathers; but he sat huge in his castle, and the screen gave a background image of crags and a glacier.

"Parliament—"

"Is still debating," Holm interrupted to finish. "The Terran Imperium has no such handicap. If you want a legal formula, well, consider us to be acting under choth law."

"The choths have no government," Vickery said, reddening.

"What is a government?" asked Liaw, Wyvan of the High Khruath—how softly!

"Why . . . well, legitimate authority—"

"Yes. The legitimacy derives, ultimately, no matter by what formula, from tradition. The authority derives, no matter by what formula, from armed force. Government is that institution which is legitimized in its use of physical coercion on the people. Have I read your human philosophers and history aright, President Vickery?"

"Well . . . yes . . . but—"

"You seem to have forgotten for the moment that the choths have been no more unanimous than your human factions," Liaw said. "Believe me, they have been divided and they are. Though a majority voted for the latest defense measures, a vocal minority has opposed: feeling, as you do, President Vickery, that the danger has been exaggerated and does not justify lifting that great a load."

Liaw sat silent for a space, during which the rest of them heard wind whistle behind him and saw a pair of his grandsons fly past. One bore the naked sword which went from house to house as a summons to war, the other a blast rifle.

The High Wyvan said: "Three choths refused to make their gift. My fellows and I threatened to call Oherran on them. Had they not yielded, we would have done so. We consider the situation to be that grave."

Holm choked. *He never told me before!— Of course he wouldn't have.* Ferune grew nearly as still on his bench as Liaw. Vickery drew breath; sweat broke out on his smoothness; he dabbed at it.

*I can almost sympathize,* Holm thought. *Suddenly getting bashed with reality like that.*

Matthew Vickery should have stayed a credit analyst instead of going into politics (Holm's mind rambled on, at the back of its own shocked alertness). Then he'd have been harmless, in fact useful; interspecies economics is often a wonderland in need of all the study anyone can give it. The trouble was, on a thinly settled globe like Avalon, government never had been too important aside from basic issues of ecology and defense. In recent decades its functions had dwindled still further, as human society changed under Ythrian influence. (A twinge of pain.) Voting was light for offices that looked merely managerial. Hence the more reactionary humans were able to elect Vickery, who Viewed With Alarm the trend toward Ythrianization. (Was no alarm justified?) He had nothing else to offer, in these darkening times.

"You understand this is confidential," Liaw said. "If word got about, the choths in question would have to consider it a deathpride matter."

"Yes," Vickery whispered.

Another silence. Holm's cigar had burned short, was scorching his fingers. He stubbed it out. It stank. He started a new one. *I smoke too much,* he thought. *Drink too much also, maybe, of late. But the work's getting done, as far as circumstance allows.*

Vickery wet his lips. "This puts . . . another complexion on affairs, doesn't it?" he said. "May I speak plainly? I must know if this is a hint that . . . you may come to feel yourselves compelled to a *coup d'état.*"

"We have better uses for our energies," Liaw told him. "Your efforts in Parliament could be helpful."

"Well—you realize I can't surrender my principles. I must be free to speak."

"It is written in the Compact," Ferune said, and his quotation did not seem superfluous even by Ythrian standards, " 'Humans inhabiting Avalon have the deathpride right of free speech, publication, and broadcast, limited only by the deathpride rights of privacy and honor and by the requirements of protection against foreign enemies.' "

"I meant—" Vickery swallowed. But he had not been years in politics for nothing. "I meant simply that friendly criticism and suggestions will always be in order," he said with most of his accustomed ease. "However, we certainly cannot risk a civil war. Shall we discuss details of a policy of nonpartisan cooperation?"

Behind the ready words, fear could still be sensed. Holm imagined he could almost read Vickery's mind, reviewing the full significance of what Liaw had said.

\* \* \*

How shall a fierce, haughty, intensely clannish and territorial race regulate its public business?

Just as on Terra, different cultures on Ythri at different periods in their histories have given a variety of answers, none wholly satisfactory or permanently enduring. The Planha speakers happened to be the most wealthy and progressive when the first explorers arrived; one is tempted to call them "Hellenistic." Eagerly adopting modern technology, they soon absorbed others into their system while modifying it to suit changed conditions.

This was the easier because the system did not

require uniformity. Within its possessions—whether these were scattered or a single block of land or sea—a choth was independent. Tradition determined what constituted a choth, though this was a tradition which slowly changed itself, as every living usage must. Tribe, anarchism, despotism, loose federation, theocracy, clan, extended family, corporation, on and on through concepts for which there are no human words, a choth ran itself.

Mostly, internal ordering was by custom and public opinion rather than by prescription and force. After all, families rarely lived close together; hence friction was minimal. The commonest sanction was a kind of weregild, the most extreme was enslavement. In between was outlawry; for some specified period, which might run as high as life, the wrongdoer could be killed by anyone without penalty, and to aid him was to incur the same punishment. Another possible sentence was exile, with outlawry automatic in case of return before the term was up. This was harsh to an Ythrian. On the other hand, the really disaffected could easily leave home (how do you fence in the sky?) and apply for membership in a choth more to their taste.

Now of course some recognized body had to try cases and hand down judgments. It must likewise settle interchoth disputes and establish policies and undertakings for the common weal. Thus in ancient times arose the Khruath, a periodic gathering of all free adults in a given territory who cared to come. It had judicial and limited legislative authority, but no administrative. The winners of lawsuits, the successful promoters of schemes and ordinances, must depend on willingness to comply or on what strength they could muster to enforce.

As Planha society expanded, regional meetings like this began to elect delegates to Year-Khruaths, which drew on larger territories. Finally these, in turn, sent

their representatives to the High Khruath of the whole
planet, which met every six years plus on extraordinary
occasions. On each level, a set of presiding officers,
the Wyvans, were chosen. These were entrusted with
explication of the laws (i.e., customs, precedents, decisions) and with trial of as many suits as possible. It
was not quite a soviet organization, because any free
adult could attend a Khruath on any level he wished.

The arrangement would not have worked on
Terra—where a version of it appeared once, long ago,
and failed bloodily. But Ythrians are less talkative, less
busybody, less submissive to bullies, and less chronically crowded than man. Modern communications, computers, information retrieval, and educational techniques
helped the system spread planetwide, ultimately
Domain-wide.

Before it reached that scale, it had had to face the
problem of administration. Necessary public works
must be funded; in theory the choths made free gifts
to this end, in practice the cost required allocation.
Behavior grossly harmful to the physical or social environment must be enjoined, however much certain
choths might profit by it or regard it as being of their
special heritage. Yet no machinery existed for compul-
sion, nor would Ythrians have imagined establishing any—
as such.

Instead, it came slowly about that when a noncom-
pliance looked important, the Wyvans of the appropriate Khruath cried Oherran on the offenders. This,
carried out after much soul-searching and with the
gravest ceremonies, was a summons to everyone in the
territory: that for the sake of their own interests and
especially their honor, they attack the defiers of the
court.

In early times, an Oherran on a whole choth meant
the end of it—enslavement of whoever had not been
slaughtered, division of holdings among the victors.
Later it might amount to as little as the arrest and

exile of named leaders. But always it fell under the concept of deathpride. If the call to Oherran was rejected, as had happened when the offense was not deemed sufficient to justify the monstrosity of invasion, then the Wyvans who cried it had no acceptable alternative to suicide.

Given the Ythrian character, Oherran works about as well as police do among men. If your society has not lost morale, human, how often must you call the police?

None who knew Liaw of The Tarns imagined he would untruthfully say that he had threatened to rip Avalon asunder.

# VI

WHERE the mighty Sagittarius flows into the Gulf of Centaurs, Avalon's second city—the only one besides Gray which rated the name—had arisen as riverport, seaport, spaceport, industrial center, and mart. Thus Centauri was predominantly a human town, akin to many in the Empire, thronged, bustling, noisy, cheerfully corrupt, occasionally dangerous. When he went there, Arinnian most of the time had to be Christopher Holm, in behavior as well as name.

Defense business now required it. He was not astonished at becoming a top officer of the West Coronan home guard, after that took its loose shape—not in a society where nepotism was the norm. It did surprise him that he seemed to be doing rather well, even enjoying himself in a grim fashion, he who had always scoffed at the "herd man." In a matter of weeks he got large-scale drills going throughout his district and was well along on the development of doctrine, communications, and supply. (Of course, it helped that most Avalonians were enthusiastic hunters, often in large groups on battues; and that the Troubles had left a military tradition not difficult to revive; and that old Daniel was on hand to advise.) Similar organizations had sprung up everywhere else. They needed to coordinate their efforts with the measures being taken by the Seamen's Brotherhood. A conference was called. It worked hard and accomplished as many of its purposes as one could reasonably hope.

Afterward Arinnian said, "Hrill, would you like to go out and celebrate? W-we may not have a lot more chances." He did not speak on impulse. He had debated it for the past couple of days.

Tabitha Falkayn smiled. "Sure, Chris. Everybody else will be."

They walked down Livewell Street. Her arm was in his; in the subtropical heat he was aware of how their skins traded sweat. "I . . . well, why do you generally call me by my human name?" he asked. "And talk Anglic to me?"

"We are humans, you and I. We haven't the feathers to use Planha as it ought to be used. Why do you mind?"

For a moment he floundered. *That personal a question . . . an insult, except between the closest friends, when it becomes an endearment. . . . No, I suppose she's just thinking human again.* He halted and swept his free hand around. "Look at that and stop wondering," he said. Instantly he feared he had been too curt.

But the big blond girl obeyed. This part of the street ran along a canal, which was oily and littered with refuse, burdened with barges, walled in by buildings jammed together, whose dingy façades reared ten or twelve stories into night heaven. Stars and the white half-disk of Morgana were lost behind the glare, blink, leap and worm-crawl of raw-colored signs. (GROG HARBOR, DANCE, EAT, GENUINE TERRAN SENSIES, FUN HOUSE, SWITCH TO MARIA JUANAS, GAMBLING, NAKED GIRLS, LOANS, BUY . . . BUY . . . BUY . . .) Groundbugs filled the roadway, pedestrians the sidewalks, a sailor, a pilot, a raftman, a fisher, a hunter, a farmer, a whore, a secretary, a drunk about to collapse, another drunk getting belligerent at a monitor, a man gaunt and hairy and ragged who stood on a corner and shouted of some obscure salvation, endless human seething, shrilling, chattering, through engine rumble, foot shuffle, raucousness blared out of loudspeakers. The air stank, dirt, smoke, oil, sewage, flesh, a breath from surrounding swamplands which would there have been a clean rotting but here was somehow made nasty.

Tabitha smiled at him anew. "Why, I call this fun, Chris," she said. "What else've we come for?"

"You wouldn't—" he stammered. "I mean, somebody like you?"

He realized he was gaping at her. Both wore thin shortsleeved blouses, kilts, and sandals; garments clung to wet bodies. But despite the sheen of moisture and the odor of female warmth that he couldn't help noticing, she stood as a creature of sea and open skies.

"Sure, what's wrong with once-in-a-while vulgarity?" she said, still amiable. "You're too puritan, Chris."

"No, no," he protested, now afraid she would think him naive. "Fastidious, maybe. But I've often been here and, uh, enjoyed myself. What I was trying to explain was, uh, I, I'm proud to belong to a choth and not proud that members of my race elect to live in a sty. Don't you see, this is the old way, that the pioneers wanted to escape."

Tabitha said a word. He was staggered. Eyath would never have spoken thus. The girl grinned. "Or, if you prefer, 'nonsense,'" she continued. "I've read Falkayn's writings. He and his followers wanted not one thing except unmolested elbow room." Her touch nudged him along. "How about that dinner we were aimed at?" Numbly, he moved.

He recovered somewhat in the respectable dimness of the Phoenix House. Among other reasons, he admitted to himself, the room was cool and her clothes didn't emphasize her shape as they did outside.

The place had live service. She ordered a catflower cocktail. He didn't. "C'mon," she said. "Unbuckle your shell."

"No, thanks, really." He found words. "Why dull my perceptions at a happy moment?"

"Seems I've heard that line before. A Stormgate saying?"

"Yes. Though I didn't think they used drugs much in Highsky either."

"They don't. Barring the sacred revels. Most of us keep to the Old Faith, you know." Tabitha regarded him awhile. "Your trouble, Chris, is you try too hard. Relax. Be more among your own species. How many humans do you have any closeness to? Bloody-gut few, I'll bet."

He bridled. "I've seen plenty of late."

"Yeh. And emergency or no, doesn't it feel good? I wouldn't try to steer somebody else's life, of course, nor am I hinting it's true of you—but fact is, a man or woman who tries to be an Ythrian is a rattlewing."

"Well, after three generations you may be restless in your choth," he said, gauging his level of sarcasm as carefully as he was able. "You've knocked around quite a bit in human country, haven't you?"

She nodded. "Several years. Itinerant huntress, trapper, sailor, prospector, over most of Avalon. I got the main piece of my share in the stake that started Draun and me in business— I got that at assorted poker tables." She laughed. "Damn, sometimes it is easier to say things in Planha!" Serious: "But remember, I was young when my parents were lost at sea. An Ythrian family adopted me. They encouraged me to take a wandertime; that's Highsky custom. If anything, my loyalty and gratitude to the choth were strengthened. I simply, well, I recognize I'm a member who happens to be human. As such, I've things to offer which—" She broke off and turned her head. "Ah, here comes my drink. Let's talk trivia. I do get starved for that on St. Li."

"I believe I will have a drink too," Arinnian said.

He found it helpful. Soon they were cheerily exchanging reminiscences. While she had doubtless led a more adventurous life than he, his had not been dull. On occasion, such as when he hid from his parents in the surf-besieged Shielding Islands, or when he had to meet a spathodont on the ground with no more than a spear because his companion lay wing-broken, he may have been in worse danger than any she had met. But he found she was most taken by his quieter memories. She had never been offplanet, except for one vacation trip to Morgana. He, son of a naval officer, had had ample chances to see the whole Lauran System from sun-wracked Elysium, through the multiple moons of Camelot, out to dark, comet-haunted Utgard. Speaking of the frigid blue peace of Phaeacia, he chanced to quote some Homeric lines, and she was delighted and wanted more and asked what else this Homer fellow had written, and the conversation turned to books. . . .

The meal was mixed, as cuisine of both races tended increasingly to be: piscoid-and-tomato chowder, beef-and-shua pie, salad of clustergrain leaf, pears, coffee spiced with witchroot. A bottle of vintage dago gave merriment. At the end, having seen her indulge the vice before, Arinnian was not shocked when Tabitha lit her pipe. "What say we look in on the Nest?" she proposed. "Might find Draun." Her partner was her superior in the guard; she was in Centauri as his aide.

But the choth concept of rank was at once more complex and more flexible than the Technic.

"Well . . . all right," Arinnian answered.

She cocked her head. "Reluctant? I'd've guessed you'd prefer the Ythrian hangout to anyplace else in town." It included the sole public house especially for ornithoids, they being infrequent here.

He frowned. "I can't help feeling that tavern is wrong. For them," he added in haste. "I'm no prude, understand."

"Yet you don't mind when humans imitate Ythrians. Uh-uh. Can't have it on both wings, son." She stood. "Let's take a glance into the Nest boozeria, a drink if we meet a friend or a good bard is reciting. Afterward a dance club, him?"

He nodded, glad—amidst an accelerating pulse—that her mood remained light. While no machinery would let them take part in the Ythrian aerial dances, moving across a floor in the arms of another bird was nearly as fine, perhaps. And, while that was as far as such contact had ever gone for him, maybe Tabitha—for she was indeed Tabitha on this steamy night, not Hrill of the skies—

He had heard various muscular oafs talk of encounters with bird girls, less boastfully than in awe. To Arinnian and his kind, their female counterparts were comrades, sisters. But Tabitha kept emphasizing his and her humanness.

They took a taxibug to the Nest, which was the tallest building in the city, and a gravshaft to its rooftop since neither had brought flying gear. Unwalled, the tavern was protected from rain by a vitryl canopy through which, at this height, stars could be seen regardless of the electric lunacy below. Morgana was sinking toward the western bottomlands, though it still silvered river and Gulf. Thunderheads piled in the east, and a rank breeze carried the mutter of the lightning that shivered in them. Insectoids circled the dim fluoroglobe set on every table. Business was sparse, a few shadowy forms perched on stools before glasses or narcobraziers, a service robot trundling about, the recorded twangs of a steel harp.

"Scum-dull," Tabitha said, disappointed. "But we can make a circuit."

They threaded among the tables until Arinnian halted and exclaimed, "Hoy-ah! Vodan, ekh-hirr."

His chothmate looked up, plainly taken aback. He was seated at drink beside a shabby-plumed female, who gave the newcomers a sullen stare.

"Good flight to you," Arinnian greeted in Planha; but what followed, however automatic, was too obvious for anything save Anglic. "I didn't expect to find you here."

"And to you, good landing," Vodan replied. "I report to my ship within hours. My transport leaves from Halcyon Island base. I came early so as not to risk being detained by a storm; we've had three whirl-devils in a row near home."

"You are yare for battle, hunter," said Tabitha at her most carefully courteous.

*That's true,* Arinnian thought. *He's ablaze to fight. Only ... if he couldn't stay with Eyath till the last minute, at least I'd've supposed he'd've been in flight-under-moon, meditating—or, anyhow, at carouse among friends—* He made introductions.

Vodan jerked a claw at his attendant. "Quenna," he said. His informality was a casual insult. She hunched between her wings, feathers erected in forlorn self-assertion.

Arinnian could think of no excuse not to join the party. He and the girl seated themselves as best they could. When the robot rolled up, they ordered thick, strong New African beer.

"How blows your wind?" Tabitha asked, puffing hard on her pipe.

"Well, as I would like for you," Vodan answered

correctly. He turned to Arinnian and, if his enthusiasm was a touch forced, it was nonetheless real. "You doubtless know I've been on training maneuvers these past weeks."

*Yes. Eyath told me more than once.*

"This was a short leave. My craft demands skill. Let me tell you about her. One of the new torpedo launchers, rather like a Terran Meteor, hai, a beauty, a spear! Proud I was to emblazon her hull with three golden stars."

*"Eyath" means "Third Star."*

Vodan went on. Arinnian glanced at Tabitha. She and Quenna had locked their gazes. Expressions billowed and jerked across the feathers; even he could read most of the unspoken half-language.

*Yes, m' sweet, you long yellow Walker born, Quenna is what she is and who're you to look down that jutting snout of yours? What else could I be, since I, growing from cub to maiden, found my lovetimes coming on whenever I thought about 'em and knew there'd never be any decent place for me in the whole universe? Oh, yes, yes, I've heard it before, don't bother: "medical treatment; counseling."—*

*Well, flabbyflesh, for your information, the choths don't often keep a weakling, and I'll not whine for help. Quenna'll lay her own course, better'n you, who're really like me . . . aren't you, now, she-human?*

Tabitha leaned forward, patted one of those arms with no heed for the talons, smiled into the reddened eyes and murmured, "Good weather for you, lass."

Astounded, Quenna reared back. For an instant she seemed about to fly at the girl, and Arinnian's hand dropped to his knife. Then she addressed Vodan: "Better we be going."

"Not yet." The Ythrian had fairly well overcome his embarrassment. "The clouds alone will decide when I see my brother again."

"We better go," she said lower. Arinnian caught the

first slight musky odor. At the next table, another male raised his crest and swiveled his head in their direction.

Arinnian could imagine the conflict in Vodan—dismiss her, defy her, strike her; no killing, she being unarmed—and yet that would be a surrender in itself, less to tradition than to mere conventionality— "We'll have to leave ourselves, soon's we finish these beers," the man said. "Glad to've come on you. Fair winds forever."

Vodan's relief was unmistakable. He mumbled through the courtesies and flapped off with Quenna. The city swallowed them.

Arinnian wondered what to say. He was grateful for the dull light; his face felt hotter than the air. He stared outward.

Tabitha said at length, softly, "That poor lost soul."

"Who, the nightflyer?" All at once he was furious. "I've met her sort before. Degenerates, petty criminals. Pray Vodan doesn't get his throat cut in whatever filthy crib she's taking him to. I know what must've happened here. He was wandering around lonely, at loose ends, a mountaineer who'd probably never come on one like her. She zeroed in, hit him with enough pheromone to excite—ugh!"

"Why should you care? I mean, of course he's a friend of yours, but I hardly believe that pathetic creature will dare try more than wheedling a tip out of him." Tabitha drank smoke. "You know," she said thoughtfully, "here's a case of Ythrian cultural lag. They've been affected by human ideas to the point where they don't give their abnormals a quick death. But they're still not interested in sponsoring rehabilitation or research on cures, or in simple charity. Someday—"

He scarcely heard the last remark. "Vodan's to marry Eyath," he said through the interior grip on his gullet.

Tabitha raised her brows. "Oh? That one you mentioned to me? Well, don't you suppose, if she heard, she'd be glad he's gotten a bit of unimportant fun and forgetting?"

"It's not right! She's too clean. She—" Arinnian gulped. Abruptly he thought: *So why not take the risk? Now I need forgetting myself.* "Is the matter small to you?" he blurted. "In that case, let's us do the same."

"Hm?" She considered him for a while that grew. Lightning moved closer on heavy gusts. His rage ebbed and he must fight not to lower his eyes, not to cringe.

At last: "You are bitter for certain, aren't you, Chris?" A chuckle. "But likewise you're hopeful."

"I'm sorry," he got out. "I n-n-never meant disrespect. I wanted to give you a, an imaginary example—make you understand why I'm upset."

"I might resent your calling it imaginary," she smiled, though her tone had become more compassionate than teasing, "except I assume it wasn't really. The answer is no, thanks."

"I expected that. We birds—" He couldn't finish, but stared down into his mug until he lifted it for a quick, deep draft.

"What d'you mean, 'we'?" she challenged.

"Why, we . . . our generation, at least—"

When she nodded, her locks caught what illumination there was. "I know," she said gravely. "That behavior pattern, promiscuous as kakkelaks provided they don't much respect their partners, but hardly able to touch birds of the opposite sex. You're a bright lad, Chris; Avalonians aren't given to introspection, but you must have some idea of the cause. Don't you want a wife and children, ever?"

"Of course. I—of course. I will."

"Most of them will, I'm sure. Most of the earlier ones did eventually, when they'd come to terms with themselves. Besides, the situation's not universal. We birds do have this in common, that we tolerate less prying than the average human. So comparative statistics aren't available. Also, the problem has gotten conspicuous these days for no deeper reason than that the movement into the choths has begun snowballing. And, finally, Chris, your experience is limited. How many out of thousands do you know well enough to describe their private lives? You'd naturally tend to be best acquainted with your own sort, especially since we birds have gotten pretty good at picking up face and body cues."

Tabitha's pipe had gone out. She emptied it and finished: "I tell you, your case isn't near as typical as you think, nor near as serious. But I do wish that going bird didn't make otherwise sensible people lose years in thwarting themselves."

Anger pricked him again. What call had she to act superior? "Now wait—" he began.

Tabitha knocked back her beer and rose. "I'm headed for my hotel," she said.

He stared up at her. "What?"

She ruffled his hair. "I'm sorry. But I'm afraid if we continue tonight, we'll brew one cyclone of a squabble. I think too well of you to want that. We'll take another evening soon if you like. Now I aim to get into bed and have Library Central screen me some of that Homer stuff."

He couldn't dissuade her. Perhaps he took most umbrage at how calm his arguments left her. When he had bidden her a chill goodnight, he slouched to the nearest phoneboard.

The first woman he called was at work. Defense production was running at seven hours on, fifteen and the odd minutes off, plus overtime. The second female acquaintance said frantically that her husband was home if that was the party he wanted; he apologized for punching a wrong number. The third was available.

She was overly plump, chattered without cease, and had the brains of a barysauroid. But what the chaos?

—He awoke about the following sunset. She was sweating in her sleep, breath stale from alcohol. He wondered why the air had gone hot and sticky. Breakdown in the conditioner? Or, hm, it'd been announced that if force screens must be raised, the power drain would require Environmental Control to shut off—

Force screens!

Arinnian jumped from bed. Rain had given way to low overcast, but he glimpsed shimmers across that slatiness. He groped through the dusty clutter in the room and snapped on the holovid.

A recording played, over and over, a man's voice high-pitched and his face stretched out of shape: "—war declared. A courier from Ythri has delivered the news in Gray, that Terra has served notice of war."

# VII

"OUR basic strategy is simple," Admiral Cajal had explained. "I would prefer a simpler one yet: pitched battle between massed fleets, winner takes all."

"But the Ythrians will scarcely be that obliging," Governor Saracoglu remarked.

"No. They aren't well organized for it, in the first place. Not in character for them to centralize operations. Besides, they must know they're foredoomed to lose any standup fight. They lack the sheer numerical strength. I expect they'll try to maintain hedgehog positions. From those they'd make sallies, harass, annihilate what smaller units of ours they found, prey on our supply lines. We can't drive straight into the Domain with that sort of menace at our rear. Prohibitively costly. We could suffer actual disaster if we let ourselves get caught between their inner and outer forces."

"Ergo, we start by capturing their advanced bases."

"The major ones. We needn't worry about tiny new colonies or backward allies, keeping a few ships per planet." Cajal gestured with a flashbeam. It probed into the darkness of a display tank, wherein gleamed points of luminance that represented the stars of this region. They crowded by thousands across those few scaled-down parsecs, a fire-swarm out of which not many men could have picked an individual. Cajal realized his talent for doing this had small intrinsic value. The storage and processing of such data were for computers. But it was an outward sign of an inner gift.

"Laura the nearest," he said. "Hru and Khrau further on, forming a triangle with it. Give me those, and I'll undertake to proceed directly against Quetlan. That should force them to call in everything they have, to protect the home star! And, since my rear and my lines will then be reasonably secure, I'll get the decisive battle I want."

"Um-m-m." Saracoglu rubbed his massive chin. Bristles made a scratchy sound; as hard as he had been at work, he kept forgetting to put on fresh inhibitor after a depilation. "You'll hit Laura first?"

"Yes, of course. Not with the whole armada. We'll split, approximately into thirds. The detached sections will proceed slowly toward Hru and Khrau, but not attack until Laura has been reduced. The force should be ample in all three systems, but I want to get the feel of Ythrian tactics—and, too, make sure they haven't some unpleasant surprise tucked under their tailfeathers."

"They might," Saracoglu said. "You know our intelligence on them leaves much to be desired. The

problems of spying on nonhumans— And Ythrian traitors are almost impossible to find, competent ones
completely impossible."

"I still don't see why you couldn't get agents into
that mostly human settlement at Laura."

"We did, Admiral, we did. But in a set of small,
close-knit communities they could accomplish nothing
except report what was publicly available to see. You
must realize, Avalonian humans no longer think, talk,
even walk quite like any Imperial humans. Imitating
them isn't feasible. And, again, deplorably few can be
bought. Furthermore, the Avalonian Admiralty is
excellent on security measures. The second in command, chap named Holm, seems to have made several
extended trips through the Empire, official and unofficial, in earlier days. I understand he did advanced study
at one of our academies. He knows our methods."

"*I* understand he's caused not just the Lauran fleet
but the planetary defenses to be enormously increased,
these past years," Cajal said. "Yes, we must certainly
take care of him first."

—That had been weeks ago. On this day (clock concept in unending starry night) the Terrans neared their
enemy.

Cajal sat alone in the middle of the superdreadnaught
*Valenderay*. Communication screens surrounded him,
and humming silence, and radial kilometers of metal,
machinery, weapons, armor, energies, through which
passed several thousand living beings. But he was, for
this moment, conscious only of what lay outside. A
viewscreen showed him: darkness, diamond hordes,
and Laura, tiny at nineteen astronomical units' remove
but gold and shining, shining.

The ships had gone out of hyperdrive and were
accelerating sunward on gravity thrust. Most were far
ahead of the flag vessel. A meeting with the defenders
could be looked for at any minute.

Cajal's mouth tightened downward at the right corner. He was a tall man, gaunt, blade-nosed, his widow's peak hair and pointed beard black though he neared his sixties. His uniform was as plain as his rank allowed.

He had been chain-smoking. Now he pulled the latest cigaret from a scorched mouth and ground it out as if it were vermin. *Why can't I endure these final waits?* he thought. *Because I will be safe while I send men to war?*

His glance turned to a picture of his dead wife, standing before their house among the high trees of Vera Fé. He moved to animate but, instead, switched on a recorder.

Music awoke, a piece he and she had loved, wellnigh forgotten on Terra but ageless in its triumphant serenity, Bach's Passacaglia. He leaned back, closed his eyes and let it heal him. *Man's duty in this life*, he thought, *is to choose the lesser evil.*

A buzz snapped him to alertness. The features of his chief executive captain filled a screen and stated, "Sir, we have received and confirmed a report of initial hostilities from Vanguard Squadron Three. No details."

"Very good, Citizen Feinberg," Cajal said. "Let me have any hard information immediately."

It would soon come flooding in, beyond the capacity of a live brain. Then it must be filtered through an intricate complex of subordinates and their computers, and he could merely hope the digests which reached him bore some significant relationship to reality. But those earliest direct accounts were always subtly helpful, as if the tone of a battle were set at its beginning.

"Aye, sir." The screen blanked.

Cajal turned off the music. "Farewell for now," he whispered, and rose. There was one other personal item in the room, a crucifix. He removed his bonnet, knelt, and signed himself. "Father, forgive us what we are about to do," he begged. "Father, have mercy on all who die. All."

"Word received, Marchwarden," the Ythrian voice announced. "Contact with Terrans, about 12 a.u. out, direction of the Spears. Firing commenced on both sides, but seemingly no losses yet."

"My thanks. Please keep me informed." Daniel Holm turned off the intercom.

"As if it were any use for me to know!" He groaned.

His mind ran through the calculation. Light, radio, neutrinos take about eight minutes to cross an astronomical unit. The news was more than an hour and a half old. That initial, exploratory fire-touch of a few small craft might well be ended already, the fragments of the vanquished whirling away on crazy orbits while the victors burned fuel as if their engines held miniature suns, trying to regain a kinetic velocity that would let them regroup. Or if other units on either side were not too distant, they might have joined in, sowing warheads wider and wider across space.

He spoke an obscenity and beat fist on palm. "If we could hypercommunicate—" But that wasn't practical. The "instantaneous" pulses of a vessel quantum-jumping around nature's speed limit could be modulated to send a message a light-year or so—however, not this deep in a star's distorting gravitational field, where you risked annihilation if you tried to travel nonrelativistically—of course, you could get away with it if you were absolutely sure of your tuning, but nobody was in wartime—and anyhow, given that capability, the Terrans would be a still worse foe, fighting them would be hopeless rather than half hopeless—*why am I rehearsing this muck?*

"And Ferune's there and I'm here!"

He sprang from his desk, stamped to the window and stood staring. A cigar fumed volcanic between his teeth. The day beyond was insultingly beautiful. An autumn breeze carried odors of salt up from the bay, which glittered and danced under Laura and heaven; and it bore scents from the gardens it passed, brilliant around their houses. North-shore hills lay in a blue haze of distance. Overhead skimmed wings. He didn't notice.

Rowena came to him. "You knew you had to stay, dear," she said. She was still auburn-maned, still slim and erect in her coverall.

"Yeh. Backup. Logistic, computer, communications support. And maybe Ferune understands space warfare better, but I'm the one who really built the planetary defense. We agreed, months back. No dishonor to me, that I do the sensible thing." Holm swung toward his wife. He caught her around the waist. "But oh, God, Ro, I didn't think it'd be this hard!"

She drew his head down onto her shoulder and stroked the grizzled hair.

Ferune of Mistwood had planned to bring his own mate along. Wharr had traveled beside him throughout a long naval career, birthed and raised their children on the homeships that accompanied every Ythrian fleet, drilled and led gun crews. But she fell sick and the medics weren't quite able to ram her through to recovery before the onslaught came. You grow old, puzzlingly so. He missed her sternness.

But he was too busy to dwell on their goodbyes. More and more reports were arriving at his flagship. A pattern was beginning to emerge.

"Observe," he said. The computers had just corrected the display tank according to the latest data. It indicated sun, planets, and color-coded sparks which stood for ships. "Combats here, here, here. Elsewhere, neutrino emissions reaching our detectors, cross-correlations getting made, fixes being obtained."

"Foully thin information," said the feathers and attitude of his aide.

"Thus far, aye, across interplanetary distances. However, we can fill in certain gaps with reason, if we assume their admiral is competent. I feel moderately sure that his pincer has but two claws, coming in almost diametrically opposite, from well north and south of the ecliptic plane . . . so." Ferune pointed. "Now he must have reserves further out. To avoid making a wide circuit with consequent risk of premature detection, these must have run fairly straight from the general direction of Pax. And were I in charge, I would have them near the ecliptic. Hence we look for their assault, as the pincers close, from here." He indicated the region.

They stood alone in the command bridge, broad though the chamber was. Ythrians wanted room to stretch their wings. Yet they were wholly linked to the ship by her intercoms, calculators, officers, crewfolk, more tenuously linked to that magnificence which darkened and bejeweled a viewscreen, where the killing had begun. Clangor and clatter of activity came faint to them, through a deep susurrus of power. The air blew warm, ruffling their plumes a little, scented with perfume of cinnamon bush and amberdragon. Blood odors would not be ordered unless and until the vessel got into actual combat; the crew would soon be worn out if stimulated too intensely.

Ferune's plan did not call for hazarding the superdreadnaught this early. Her power belonged in his end game. At that time he intended to show the Terrans why she was called after the site of an ancient battle on Ythri. He had had the Anglic translation of the name painted broad on the sides: *Hell Rock*.

A new cluster of motes appeared in the tank. Their brightnesses indicated ship types, as accurately as analysis of their neutrino emanations could suggest. The aide started. His crest bristled. "That many more hostiles, so soon? Uncle, the odds look bad."

"We knew they would. Don't let this toy hypnotize

you. I've been through worse. Half of me is regenerated tissue after combat wounds. And I'm still skyborne."

"Forgive me, Uncle, but most of your fights were police actions inside the Domain. This is the *Empire* coming."

Ferune expressed: "I am not unaware of that. And I too have studied advanced militechnics, both practical and theoretical." Aloud he said, "Computers, robots, machines are only half the makers of a warweird. There are also brains and hearts."

Claws clacked on the deck as he walked to the viewscreen and peered forth. His experienced eye picked out a glint among the stars, one ship. Otherwise his fleet was lost to vision in the immensity through which it fanned.

"A new engagement commencing," said the intercom.

Ferune waited motionless for details. Through his mind passed words from one of the old Terran books it pleasured him to read. *The fear of a king is as the roaring of a lion: whoso provoketh him to anger sinneth against his own soul.*

\* \* \*

Hours built into days while the fleets, in their hugely scattered divisions, felt for and sought each other's throats.

Consider: at a linear acceleration of one Terran gravity, a vessel can, from a "standing start," cover one astronomical unit—about 149 million kilometers—in a bit under fifty hours. At the end of that period, she has gained 1060 kilometers per second of velocity. In twice the time, she will move at twice the speed and will have spanned four times the distance. No matter what power is conferred by thermonuclear engines, no matter what maneuverability comes from a gravity thrust which reacts directly against that fabric of relationships we call space, one does not quickly alter quantities on this order of magnitude.

Then, too, there is the sheer vastness of even inter-planetary reaches. A sphere one a. u. in radius has the volume of some thirteen million million Terras; to multiply this radius by ten is to multiply the volume by a thousand. No matter how sensitive the instruments, one does not quickly scan those deeps, nor ever do it with much accuracy beyond one's immediate neighborhood, nor know where a detached object is *now* if signals are limited to light speed. As the maddeningly incomplete hoard of data grows, not just the parameters of battle calculations change; the equations do. One discovers he has lost hours in travel which has turned out to be useless or worse, and must lose hours or days more in trying to remedy matters.

But then, explosively fast, will come a near enough approach at nearly enough matched velocities for a combat which may well be finished in seconds.

\* \* \*

"Number Seven, launch!" warned the dispatcher robot, and flung *Hooting Star* out to battle.

Her engines took hold. A thrum went through the bones of Philippe Rochefort where he sat harnessed in the pilot chair. Above his instrument panel, over his helmet and past either shoulder, viewscreens filled a quarter globe with suns. Laura, radiance stopped down lest it blind him, shone among them as a minikin disk between two nacreous wings of zodiacal light.

His radar alarm whistled and lit up, swiveling an arrow inside a clear ball. His heart sprang. He couldn't help glancing that way. And he caught a glimpse of the cylinder which hurtled toward *Ansa*'s great flank.

During a launch, the negagrav screen in that area of the mother vessel is necessarily turned off. Nothing is there to repulse a torpedo. If the thing makes contact and detonates— In vacuum, several kilotons are not quite so appallingly destructive as in air or water; and a capital ship is armored and compartmented against concussion and heat, thickly shielded to cut down what hard radiation gets inside. Nevertheless she will be badly hurt, perhaps crippled, and men will be blown apart, cooked alive, shrieking their wish to die.

An energy beam flashed. An instant's incandescence followed. Sensors gave their findings to the appropriate computer. Within a millisecond of the burst, a "Cleared" note warbled. One of Wa Chaou's guns had caught the torpedo square on.

"Well done!" Rochefort cried over the intercom. "Good show, Watch Out!" He rotated his detectors in search of the boat which must have been sufficiently close to loose that missile.

Registry. Lockon. *Hooting Star* surged forward. *Ansa* dwindled among the constellations. "Give me an estimated time to come in range, Abdullah," Rochefort said.

"He seems aware of us," Helu's voice answered, stonecalm. "Depends on whether he'll try to get away or close in. . . . Um-m, yes, he's skiting for cover." (*I would too, for fair,* Rochefort thought, *when a heavy cruiser's spitting boats. That's a brave skipper who sneaked this near.*) "We can intercept in about ten minutes, assuming he's at his top acceleration. But I don't think anybody else will be able to help us, and if we wait for them, he'll escape."

"We're not waiting," Rochefort decided. He lasered his intentions back to the squadron control office aboard ship and got an okay. Meanwhile he wished his sweat were not breaking out wet and sour. He wasn't afraid, though; his pulse beat high but steady and never before had he seen the stars with such clarity and exactness. It was good to know he had the inborn courage for Academy psych-training to develop.

"If you win," SC said, "make for"—a string of

numbers which the machines memorized—"and act at discretion. We've identified a light battleship there. We and *Ganymede* between us will try saturating its defenses. Good luck."

The voice clipped off. The boat ran, faster every second until the ballistics meters advised deceleration. Rochefort heeded and tapped out the needful orders. Utterly irrelevant passed through his head the memory of an instructor's lecture. "Living pilots, gunners, all personnel, are meant to make decisions. Machines execute most of those decisions, set and steer courses, lay and fire guns, faster and more precisely than nerve or muscle. Machines, consciousness-level computers, could also be built to decide. They have been, in the past. But while their logical abilities might be far in excess of yours and mine, they always lacked a certain totality, call it intuition or insight or what you will. Furthermore, they were too expensive to use in war in any numbers. You, gentlemen, are multipurpose computers who have a *reason* to fight and survive. Your kind is abundantly available and, apart from programming, can be produced in nine months by unskilled labor." Rochefort remembered telling lower classmen that it was three demerits if you didn't laugh at the hoary joke.

"Range," Helu said.

Energy beams stabbed. The scattered, wasted photons which burned along their paths were the barest fraction of the power within.

One touched *Hooting Star*. The boat's automata veered her before it could penetrate her thin plating. That was a roar of sidewise thrust. The interior fields couldn't entirely compensate for the sudden high acceleration. Rochefort was crammed back against his harness till it creaked, while weight underfoot shifted dizzyingly.

It passed. Normal one-gee-down returned. They

were alive. They didn't even seem to need a patchplate; if they had been pierced, the hole was small enough for self-sealing. And yonder in naked-eye sight was the enemy!

With hands and voice, Rochefort told his boat to drive straight at that shark shape. It swelled monstrously fast. Two beams lanced from it and struck. Rochefort held his vector constant. He was hoping Wa Chaou would thus be able to get a fix on their sources and knock them out before they could do serious damage. *Flash! Flash!* Brightness blanked. "Oh, glorious! Ready torps."

The Ythrian drew nearer till the human could see a painted insigne, a wheel whose spokes were flower petals. *That's right, they put personal badges on their lesser craft, same as we give unofficial names. Wonder what that'n means.* He'd been told that some of their speedsters carried ball guns. But hard objects cast in your path weren't too dangerous till relative velocities got into the tens of KPS.

She fired a torpedo. Wa Chaou wrecked it almost in its tube. *Hooting Star's* slammed home.

The explosion was at such close quarters that its fiery gases filled the Terran's screen. A fragment struck her. She shivered and belled. Then she was past, alone in clean space. Her opponent was a cloud which puffed outward till it grew invisible, a few seared chunks of metal and possibly bone cooling off to become meteoroids, falling away aft, gone from sight in seconds.

"If you will pardon the expression," Rochefort said shakily, "yahoo!"

"That was a near one," Helu said. "We'd better ask for antirad boosters when we get back."

"Uh-huh. Right now, though, we've unfinished business." Rochefort instructed the boat to change vectors. "No fears, after the way you chaps conducted yourselves."

They were not yet at the scene when joyful broadcasts and another brief blossoming told them that a hornet swarm of boats and missiles had stung the enemy battleship to death.

# VIII

SLOWLY those volumes of space wherein the war was being fought contracted and neared each other. At no time were vessels ranked. Besides being unfeasible to maintain, formations tight and rigid would have invited a nuclear barrage. At most, a squadron of small craft might travel in loose echelon for a while. If two major units of a flotilla came within a hundred kilometers, it was reckoned close. However, the time lag of communication dropped toward zero, the reliability of detection swooped upward, deadly encounters grew ever more frequent.

It became possible to know fairly well what the opponent had in play and where. It became possible to devise and guide a campaign.

Cajal remarked in a tape report to Saracoglu: "If

every Ythrian system were as strong as Laura, we
might need the whole Imperial Navy to break them.
Here they possess, or did possess, approximately half
the number of hulls that I do—which is to say, a sixth
the number we deemed adequate for handling the
entire Domain. Of course, that doesn't mean their
actual strength is in proportion. By our standards, they
are weak in heavy craft. But their destroyers, still more
their corvettes and torpedo boats, make an astonishing
total. I am very glad that no other enemy sun, besides
Quetlan itself, remotely compares with Laura!

"Nevertheless, we are making satisfactory progress.
In groundling language—a technical summary will be
appended for you—we can say that about half of what
remains to them is falling back on Avalon. We intend
to follow them there, dispose of them, and thus have
the planet at our mercy.

"The rest of their fleet is disengaging, piecemeal,
and retreating spaceward. Doubtless they mean to
scatter themselves throughout the uninhabitable planets, moons, and asteroids of the system, where they
must have bases, and carry on hit-and-run war. This
should prove more nuisance than menace, and once
we are in occupation their government will recall
them. Probably larger vessels, which have hyperdrive,
will seek to go reinforce elsewhere: again, not unduly
important.

"I am not underestimating these people. They fight
skillfully and doggedly. They must expect to use planetary defenses in conjunction with those ships moving
toward the home world. God grant, more for their
sakes than ours, most especially for the sakes of inno-
cent females and children of both races, God grant
their leaders see reason and capitulate before we hurt
them too badly."

The half disk of Avalon shone sapphire swirled with
silver, small and dear among the stars. Morgana was

coming around the dark side. Ferune remembered night flights beneath it with Wharr, and murmured, "*O moon of my delight that knows no wane—*"

"Hoy?" said Daniel Holm's face in the screen.

"Nothing. My mind drifted." Ferune drew breath. "We've skimpy time. They're coming in fast. I want to make certain you've found no serious objection to the battle plan as detailed."

The laser beam took a few seconds to flicker between flagship and headquarters. Ferune went back to his memories.

"I bugger well do!" Holm growled. "I already told you. You've brought *Hell Rock* too close in. Prime target."

"And I told you," Ferune answered, "we no longer need her command capabilities." *I wish we did, but our losses have been too cruel.* "We do need her fire power and, yes, her attraction for the enemy. That's why I never counted on getting her away to Quetlan. There she'd be just one more unit. Here she's the keystone of our configuration. If things break well, she will survive. I know the scheme is not guaranteed, but it was the best my staff, computers, and self could produce on what you also knew beforehand would be short notice. To argue, or modify much, at this late hour is to deserve disaster."

Silence. Morgana rose further from Avalon as the ship moved.

"Well ..." Holm slumped. He had lost weight till his cheekbones stood forth like ridges in upland desert. "I s'pose."

"Uncle, a report of initial contact," Ferune's aide said.

"Already?" The First Marchwarden of Avalon turned to the comscreen. "You heard, Daniel Holm? Fair winds forever." He cut the circuit before the man could reply. "Now," he told the aide, "I want a recomputation of the optimum orbit for this ship. Project the

Terran's best moves ... from their viewpoint, in the
light of what information we have ... and adjust ours
accordingly."

Space sparkled with fireworks. Not every explosion,
nor most, signified a hit; but they were thickening.

*Three Stars* slammed from her cruiser. At once her
detectors reported an object. Analysis followed within
seconds—a Terran Meteor, possible to intercept, no
nearby companions. "Quarry!" Vodan sang out. "Five
minutes to range."

A yell went through the hull. Two weeks and worse
of maneuver, cooped in metal save for rare, short
hours when the flotilla dipped into combat, had been
heavy chains to lift.

His new vector pointed straight at Avalon. The
planet waxed; he flew toward Eyath. He had no doubts
about his victory. *Three Stars* was well blooded. She
was necessarily larger than her Imperial counterpart—
Ythrian requirements for room—and therefore had a
trifle less acceleration. But her firepower could on that
account be made greater, and had been.

Vodan took feet off perch and hung in his harness.
He spread his wings. Slowly he beat them, pumping
his blood full of oxygen, his body full of strength and
swiftness. It tingled, it sang. He heard a rustling aft
as his four crewfolk did likewise. Stars gleamed above
and around him.

Three representations occupied Daniel Holm's office
and, now, his mind. A map of Avalon indicated the
ground installations. The majority were camouflaged
and, he hoped, he would have prayed if he believed,
were unknown to the enemy. Around a holographic
world globe, variegated motes swung in multitudinous
orbits. Many stations had been established a few days
ago, after being transported to their launch sites from
underground automated factories which were also

supposed to be secret. Finally a display tank indicated what was known of the shifting ships out yonder.

Holm longed for a cigar, but his mouth was too withered by too much smoke in the near past. *Crock, how I could use a drink!* he thought. Neither might that be; the sole allowable drugs were those which kept him alert without exacting too high a metabolic price.

He stared at the tank. *Yeh. They're sure anxious to nail our flagship. Really converging on her.*

He sought the window. While Gray still lay shadowy, the first dawnlight was picking out houses and making the waters sheen. Above, the sky arched purple, its stars blurred by the negagrav screens. They had to keep changing pattern, to give adequate coverage while allowing air circulation. That stirred up restless little winds, cold and a bit damp. But on the whole the country reached serene. The storms were beyond the sky and inside the flesh.

Holm was alone, more alone than ever in his life, though the forces of a world awaited his bidding. It would have to be his; the computers could merely advise. He guessed that he felt like an infantryman preparing to charge.

"There!" Rochefort shouted.

He saw a moving point of light in a viewscreen set to top magnification. It grew as he watched, a needle, a spindle, a toy, a lean sharp-snouted hunter on whose flank shone three golden stars.

The vectors were almost identical. The boats neared more slowly than they rushed toward the planet. *Odd,* Rochefort thought, *how close Ansa's come without meeting any opposition. Are they just going to offer token resistance? I'd hate to kill somebody for a token.* Avalon was utterly beautiful. He was approaching in such wise that on his left the great disk had full daylight—azure, turquoise, indigo, a thousand different blues beneath the intercurving purity of cloud, a land mass glimpsed green and brown and tawny. On his right was darkness, but moonlight shimmered mysteriously across oceans and weather.

Wa Chaou sent a probe of lightning. No result showed. The range was extreme. It wouldn't stay thus for long. Now Rochefort needed no magnification to see the hostile hull. In those screens it was as yet a glint. But it slid across the stellar background, and it was more constant than the fireballs twinkling around.

Space blazed for a thousand kilometers around that giant spheroid which was *Hell Rock*. She did not try to dodge; given her mass, that was futile. She orbited her world. The enemy ships plunged in, shot, went by and maneuvered to return. They were many, she was one, save for a cloud of attendant Meteors and Comets. Her firepower, though, was awesome; still more were her instrumental and computer capabilities. She had not been damaged. When a section of screen must be turned off to launch a pack of missiles, auxiliary energy weapons intercepted whatever was directed at the vulnerable spot.

Rays had smitten. But none could be held steady through an interval sufficient to get past those heavy plates. Bombs whose yield was lethal radiation exploded along the limits of her defense. But the gamma quanta and neutrons were drunk down by layer upon layer of interior shielding. The last of them, straggling to those deep inner sections where organic creatures toiled, were so few that ordinary medication nullified their effects.

She had been built in space and would never touch ground. A planetoid in her own right, she blasted ship after ship that dared come against her.

Cajal's Supernova was stronger. But *Valenderay* must not be risked. The whole purpose of all that armament and armor was to protect the command of a fleet. When word reached him, he studied the display tank. "We're wasting lesser craft. She eats them," he said, chiefly to himself. "I hate to send capital vessels in. The enemy seems to have much more defensive stuff than we looked for, and it's bound to open up on us soon. But that close, speed and maneuverability don't count for what they should. We must have sheer force to take that monster out; and we must do that before we can pose any serious threat to the planet." He tugged his beard. "S-s-so . . . between them, *Persei, Ursa Minor, Regulus, Jupiter,* and attendants should be able to do the job . . . fast enough and at enough of a distance that they can also cope with whatever the planet may throw."

Tactical computers ratified and expanded his decision. He issued the orders.

Vodan saw a torpedo go past. "Hai, good!" he cried. Had he applied a few megadynes less of decelerative force, that warhead would have connected. The missile braked and came about, tracking, but one of his gunners destroyed it.

The Terran boat crawled ahead, off on the left and low. Vodan's instruments reported she was exerting more sideways than forward thrust. The pilot must mean to cross the Ythrian bows, bare kilometers ahead, loose a cloud of radar window, and hope the concerted fire of his beam guns would penetrate before the other could range him. Since Ythrians, unlike Terrans, did not fight wearing spacesuits—how could anybody not go insane after more than a few hours in those vile, confining things?—a large hole in a compartment killed them.

The son-of-a-zirraukh was good, Vodan acknowledged happily. Lumbering and awkward as most space engagements were, this felt almost like being back in air. The duel had lasted until Avalon stood enormous in the bow screens. In fact, they were closer to atmosphere than was prudent at their velocity. They'd better end the affair.

Vodan saw how.

He went on slowing at a uniform rate, as if he intended presently to slant off. He thought the Terran would think: *He sees what I plan. When I blind his radar, he will sheer from my fire in an unpredictable direction. Ah, but we're not under hyperdrive. He can't move at anything like the speed of energy beams. Mine can cover the entire cone of his possible instantaneous positions.*

For that, however, the gun platform needed a constant vector. Otherwise too many unknowns entered the equations and the target had an excellent chance of escaping. For part of a minute, if Vodan had guessed right, the Meteor would forego its advantage of superior mobility. And ... he had superior weapons.

The Terran might well expect a torpedo and figure he could readily dispose of the thing. He might not appreciate how very great a concentration of energy his opponent could bring to bear for a short while, when all projectors were run at overload.

Vodan made his calculations. The gunners made their settings.

The Meteor passed ahead, dwarfish upon luminous Avalon. A sudden, glittering fog sprang from her. At explosive speed, it spread to make a curtain. And it hid one ship as well as the other.

Rays sliced through, seeking. Vodan knew exactly where to aim his. They raged for 30 seconds.

The metal dust scattered. Avalon again shone enormous and calm. Vodan ceased fire before his projectors should burn out. Nothing came from the Meteor. He used magnification, and saw the hole which gaped astern by her drive cones. Air gushed forth, water condensing ghost-white until it vanished into void. Acceleration had ended entirely.

Joy lofted in Vodan. "We've struck him!" he shouted.

"He could launch his torps in a flock," the engineer worried.

"No. Come look if you wish. His powerplant took that hit. He has nothing left except his capacitor bank. If he can use that to full effect, which I doubt, he still can't give any object enough initial velocity to worry us."

"Kh'hng. Shall we finish him off?"

"Let's see if he'll surrender. Standard band. . . . Calling Imperial Meteor. Calling Imperial Meteor."

*One more trophy for you, Eyathl.*

*Hell Rock* shuddered and toned. Roarings rolled inward. Air drifted bitter with smoke, loud with screams and bawled commands, running feet and threshing wings. Compartment after compartment was burst open to space. Bulkheads slid to seal twisted metal and tattered bodies off from the living.

She fought. She could fight on under what was left of her automata, well after the last of the crew were gone whose retreat she was covering.

Those were Ferune, his immediate staff, and a few ratings from Mistwood who had been promised the right to abide by their Wyvan. They made their way down quaking, tolling corridors. Sections lay dark where fluoropanels and facings were peeled back from the mighty skeleton.

"How long till they beat her asunder?" asked one at Ferune's back.

"An hour, maybe," he guessed. "They wrought well who built her. Of course, Avalon will strike before then."

"At what minute?"

"Daniel Holm must gauge that."

They crowded into their lifeboat. Ferune took the controls. The craft lifted against interior fields; valves swung ponderously aside; she came forth to sight of stars and streaked for home.

He glanced behind. The flagship was ragged, crumpled, cratered. In places metal had run molten till it congealed into ugliness, in other places it glowed. Had the bombardment been able to concentrate on those sites where defenses were down, a megaton warhead or two would have scattered the vessel in gas and ashes. But the likelihood of a precise hit at medium range was too slim to risk a supermissile against her remaining interception capability. Better to hold well off and gnaw with lesser blasts.

"Fare gladly into the winds," Ferune whispered. In this moment he put aside his new ways, his alien ways, and was of Ythri, Mistwood, Wharr, the ancestors and the children.

Avalon struck. The boat reeled. Under an intolerable load of light, viewscreens blanked. Briefly, illumination went out. The flyers crouched, packed together, in bellowing, heat, and blindness.

It passed. The boat had not been severely damaged. Backup systems cut in. Vision returned, inside and outside. Aft, *Hell Rock* was silhouetted against the waning luridness of a fireball that spread across half heaven.

A rating breathed, "How . . . many . . . megatons?"

"I don't know," Ferune said. "Presumably ample to dispose of those Imperials we sucked into attacking us."

"A wonder we came through," said his aide. Every feather stood erect on him and shivered.

"The gases diffused across kilometers," Ferune reminded. "We've no screen field generator here, true. But by the time the front reached us, even a velocity equivalent of several million degrees could not raise our temperature much."

Silence clapped down, while smaller detonations glittered and faded in deeper distances and energy swords lunged. Eyes sought eyes. The brains behind were technically trained.

Ferune spoke it for them. "Ionizing radiation, primary and secondary. I cannot tell how big a dose we got. The meter went off scale. But we can probably report back, at least."

He gave himself to his piloting. Wharr waited.

Rochefort groped through the hull of *Hooting Star*. Interior grav generation had been knocked out; freefalling, they were now weightless. And airless beyond the enclosing armor. Stillness pressed inward till he heard his heart as strongly as he felt it. Beads of sweat broke off brow, nose, cheeks, and danced between eyes and faceplate, catching light in oily gleams. That light fell queerly across vacuum, undiffused, sharpshadowed.

"Watch Out!" he croaked into his radio. "Watch Out, are you there?"

"I'm afraid not," said Helu's voice in his earplugs, from the engine room.

Rochefort found the little body afloat behind a panel cut half loose from its moorings. The same ray had burned through suit and flesh and out through the suit, cauterizing as it went so that only a few bloodgouts drifted around. "Wa Chaou bought it?" asked Helu.

"Yes." Rochefort hugged the Cynthian to his breast and fought not to weep.

"Any fire control left?"

"No."

"Well, I think I can squeeze capacitor power into the drive units. We can't escape the planet on that, but maybe we can land without vaporizing in transit. It'll take a pretty fabulous pilot. Better get back to your post, skipper."

Rochefort opened the helmet in order to close the bulged-out eyes, but the lids wouldn't go over them.

He secured the corpse in a bight of loose wire and returned forward to harness himself in.

The call light was blinking. Mechanically, conscious mainly of grief, he plugged a jack into his suit unit and pressed the Accept button.

Anglic, accented somehow both guttural and ringing: "—Imperial Meteor. Are you alive? This is the Avalonian. Acknowledge or we shoot."

"Ack . . . ack—" Before the noise in his throat could turn to sobbing, Rochefort said, "Yes, captain here."

"We will take you aboard if you wish."

Rochefort clung to the seatback, legs trailing aft. It hummed and crackled in his ears.

"Ythri abides by the conventions of war," said the unhuman voice. "You will be interrogated but not mistreated. If you refuse, we must take the precaution of destroying you."

*Kh-h-h-h . . . m-m-m-m. . . .*

"Answer at once! We are already too nigh Avalon. The danger of being caught in crossfire grows by the minute."

"Yes," Rochefort heard himself say. "Of course. We surrender."

"Good. I observe you have not restarted your engine. Do not. We are matching velocities. Link yourselves and jump off into space. We will lay a tractor beam on you and bring you in as soon as may be. Understood? Repeat."

Rochefort did.

"You fought well," said the Ythrian. "You showed deathpride. I shall be honored to welcome you aboard." And silence.

Rochefort called Helu. The men bent the ends of a cable around their waists, cracked the personnel lock, and prepared to tumble free. Kilometers off they saw the vessel that bore three stars, coming like an eagle.

The skies erupted in radiance.

When ragged red dazzlement had cleared from their vision, Helu choked, *"Ullah akbar, Ullah akbar. . . .* They're gone. What *was* it?"

"Direct hit," Rochefort said. Shock had blown some opening in him for numbness to drain out of. He felt strength rising in its wake. His mind flashed, fast as those war lightnings yonder but altogether cool. "They knew we were helpless and had no friends nearby. But in spite of a remark the captain made, they must've forgotten to look out for their own friends. The planet-based weapons have started shooting. I imagine the missiles include a lot of tracker torpedoes. Our engines were dead. His weren't. A torp homed on the emissions."

"What, no recognition circuits?"

"Evidently not. To lash out on the scale they seem to be doing, the Avalonians would've had to sacrifice quality for quantity, and rely on knowing the dispositions of units. It was not reasonable to expect any this close in. The fighting's further out. I daresay that torp was bound there, against some particular Imperial concentration, when it happened to pass near us."

"Um." They hung between darkness and glitter, breathing. "We've lost our ride," Helu said.

"Got to make do, then," Rochefort answered. "Come."

Beneath his regained calm, he was shaken at what appeared to be the magnitude of the Avalonian response.

# IX

**W**HEN the boat had come to rest, thundering and shuddering ended, only bake-oven heat and scorched smells remaining, Rochefort let go of awareness.

He swam up from the nothing some minutes later. Helu stood over him. "Are you okay, skipper?" At first the engineer's voice seemed to come across a whining distance, and the sweat and soot on his face blurred into the haze which grayed all vision.

"Okay," Rochefort mumbled. "Get me . . . 'nother stimpill. . . ."

Helu did, with a glass of water that wrought a miracle on wooden tongue and parchment palate. "Hand of Fatima, what a ride!" he said unevenly. "I thought for certain we were finished. How did you ever get us down?"

"I don't remember," Rochefort answered.

The drug took hold, giving him back clarity of mind and senses, plus a measure of energy. He could reconstruct what he must have done in those last wild minutes. The ergs stored in the capacitors had not been adequate to kill the boat's entire velocity relative to the planetary surface. He had used them for control, for keeping the hull from being boiled off by the atmospheric friction that braked it. *Hooting Star* had skipped halfway around the globe on the tropopause, as a stone may be skipped over a lake, then screamed down on a long slant which would have ended in drowning—for the hole aft could not be patched, and a sealed-off engine room would have weighed too much when flooded—except that somehow he, Philippe Rochefort, had spotted (he recollected now) a chain of islands and achieved a crash landing on one. . . .

He spent a while in the awe of being alive. Afterward he unharnessed, and in their separate fashions he and Helu gave thanks; and they added a wish for the soul of Wa Chaou. By that time the hull had cooled to a point where they dared touch the lock. They found its outer valve had been torn loose when the boat plowed across ground.

"Good air," Helu said.

Rochefort inhaled gratefully. It was not just that the cabin was hot and stinking. No regeneration system on any spacecraft could do the entire work of a living world. This atmosphere that streamed to meet him smelled of ozone, iodine, greenery, flower fragrances; it was mild but brisk with breezes.

"Must be about Terran standard pressure," Helu went on. "How does a planet like this keep so much gas?"

"Surely you've met the type before," Rochefort said.

"Yes, but never stopped to wonder. Now that I've

had the universe given back to me, I'd, uh, I'd like to know it better."

"Well, magnetism helps," Rochefort explained absently. "The core is small, but on the other hand the rotation is rapid, making for a reasonable value of H. Besides, the field has fewer charged particles to keep off, therefore fewer get by it to bounce off gas molecules. Likewise, the total ultraviolet and X radiation received is less. That sun's fairly close—we're getting about 10 percent more illumination than Terra does—but it's cooler than Sol. The energy distribution curve peaks at a lower frequency and the stellar wind is weak."

Meanwhile he sensed the gravity. His weight was four-fifths what it had been when the boat's interior field was set at standard pull. When you dropped sixteen kilos you noticed it at first—a bounciness, an exuberance of the body which the loss of a friend and the likelihood of captivity did not entirely quench—though you soon came to take the feeling for granted.

He stepped forth and looked around. Those viewscreens which remained functional had shown him this area was unpeopled. Inland it rose steeply. On the other side it sloped down to a beach where surf tumbled in a white violence whose noise reached him across more than a kilometer. Beyond, a syenite sea rolled to a horizon which, in spite of Avalon's radius, did not seem appreciably nearer than on Terra or Esperance. The sky above was a blue more bright and deep than he was used to. The sun was low, sinking twice as fast as on man's home. Its disk showed a bit larger, its hue was tinged golden. A sickle moon trailed, a fourth again the angular diameter of Luna seen from the ground. Rochefort knew it was actually smaller but, being close, raised twice the tides.

Occasional sparks and streaks blinked up there—monstrous explosions in space. Rochefort turned his mind from them. For him the war was presumably over. Let it be over for everybody, soon, before more consciousnesses died.

He gave his attention to the life encircling him. His vessel had gouged and charred through a dense mat of low-growing, beryl-green stuff which covered the island. "I suppose this explains why the planet has no native forests," he murmured, "which may in turn help explain why animal life is underevolved."

"Dinosaur stage?" Helu asked, watching a flock of clumsy winged creatures go by. They each had four legs; the basic vertebrate design on Avalon was hexapodal.

"Well, reptiloid, though some have developed features like hair or an efficient heart. By and large, they don't stand a chance against mammalian or avian life forms. The colonists had to do quite a lot of work to establish a stable mixed colony, and they keep a good deal of land reserved, including the whole equatorial continent."

"You've really studied them up, haven't you?"

"I was interested. And . . . seemed wrong to let them be only my targets. Seemed as if I ought to have some reality on the people I was going to fight."

Helu peered inland. Scattered shrubs and trees did exist. The latter were either low and thick or slim and supple, to survive the high winds that rapid rotation must often create. Autumn or no, many flowers continued in bloom, flamboyant scarlets and yellows and purples. Fruits clustered thick on several other kinds of plant.

"Can we eat local food?" Helu asked.

"Yes, of course," Rochefort said. "They'd never have made the success they did, colonizing, in the time they've had, if they couldn't draw on native resources. Some essentials are missing, assorted vitamins and whatnot. Imported domestic animals had to be revamped genetically on that account. We'd come down with deficiency diseases if we tried to eat Avalonian material exclusively. However, that wouldn't happen fast, and I've read that much of it is tasty. Unfortunately, I've read that much is poisonous, too, and I don't know which is which."

"Hm." Helu tugged his mustache and scowled. "We'd better call for somebody to come get us."

"No rush," said Rochefort. "Let's first learn what we can. The boat has supplies for weeks, remember. We just might be able to—" He stopped. Knowledge stung him. "Right now we've a duty."

Perforce they began by making a spade and pick out of scrap; and then the plant cover was tough and the soil beneath a stubborn clay. Sunset had perished in flame before they got Wa Chaou buried.

A full moon would have cast ample light; higher albedo as well as angular size and illumination gave it more than thrice the brilliance of Luna. Tonight's thin crescent was soon down. But the service could be read by two lamp-white companion planets and numberless stars. Most of their constellations were the same as those Rochefort had shared with Eve Davisson on Esperance. Three or four parsecs hardly count in the galaxy.

*Does a life? I must believe so.* "—Father, unto You in what form he did dream You, we commit this being our comrade; and we pray that You grant him rest, even as we pray for ourselves. Lord have mercy, Lord have mercy, Lord have mercy."

The gruesome little flashes overhead were dying away.

"Disengage," Cajal said. "Withdraw. Regroup in wide orbits."

"But, but, Admiral," protested a captain of his staff, "their ships—they'll use the chance to escape—disappear into deep space."

Cajal's glance traveled from screen to screen on the comboard. Faces looked out, some human, some

non-human, but each belonging to an officer of Imperial Terra. He found it hard to meet those eyes.

"We shall have to accept that," he told them. "What
we cannot accept is our present rate of losses. Laura
is only a prologue. If the cost of its capture proves
such that we have to wait for reinforcements, giving
Ythri time to reorganize, there goes our entire strategy. The whole war will become long and expensive."

He sighed. "Let us be frank, citizens," he said. "Our
intelligence about this system was very bad. We had
no idea what fortifications had been created for Avalon—"

\* \* \*

In orbit, automated stations by the hundreds, whose
powerplants fed no engines but, exclusively, defensive
screens and offensive projectors; thus mortally dangerous to come in range of. Shuttling between them and
the planet, hence guarded by them, a host of supply
craft, bringing whatever might be needed to keep the
robots shooting.

On the surface, and on the moon, a global grid of
detectors, launch tubes, energy weapons too immense for
spaceships to carry; some buried deep in rock or on
the ocean beds, some aboveground or afloat. The
chance of a vessel or missile getting through from
space, unintercepted, small indeed; and negafields
shielding every vital spot.

In the air, a wasp swarm of pursuit craft on patrol,
ready to streak by scores against any who was so rash
as to intrude.

\* \* \*

"—and the defenders used our ignorance brilliantly.
They lured us into configurations that allowed those
instrumentalities to inflict staggering damage. We're
mouse-trapped between the planet and their ships.
Inferior though the enemy fleet is, under present circumstances it's disproportionately effective.

"We have no choice. We must change the circumstances,

fast. If we pull beyond reach of the defenses, their fleet will again be outmatched and, I'm sure, will withdraw to the outer parts of this system as Captain K'thak has said."

"Then, sir?" asked a man. "What do we do then?"

"We make a reassessment," Cajal told him.

"Can we saturate their capabilities with what we've got on hand?" wondered another.

"I do not know," Cajal admitted.

"How could they do this?" cried a man from behind the bandages that masked him. His ship had been among those smashed. "A wretched colony—what's the population, fourteen million, mostly ranchers?—how was it possible?"

"You should understand that," Cajal reproved, though gently because he knew drugs were dulling brain as well as pain. "Given abundant nuclear energy, ample natural resources, sophisticated automatic technology, one needs nothing else except the will. Machines produce machines, exponentially. In a few years one has full production under way, limited only by available minerals; and an underpopulated, largely rural world like Avalon will have a good supply of those.

"I imagine," he mused aloud—because any thought was better than thought of what the navy had suffered this day—"that same pastoral economy simplified the job of keeping secret how great an effort was being mounted. A more developed society would have called on its existing industry, which is out in the open. The Avalonian leadership, once granted *carte blanche* by the electorate, made most of its facilities from zero, in regions where no one lives." He nodded. "Yes, citizens, let us confess we have been taken." Straightening: "Now we salvage what we can."

Discussion turned to ways and means. Battered, more than decimated, the Terran force was still gigantic. It was strewn through corresponding volumes of space, its units never motionless. Arranging for an orderly retreat was a major operation in itself. And there would be the uncertainties, imponderables, and inevitable unforeseen catastrophes of battle. And the Avalonian space captains must be presented with obvious chances to quit the fight—not mere tactical openings, but a clear demonstration that their withdrawal would not betray their folk—lest they carry on to the death and bring too many Imperials with them.

But at last the computers and underlings were at work on details, the first moves of disengagement were started. Cajal could be alone.

*Or can I be?* he thought. *Ever again? The ghosts are crowding around.*

*No.* This debacle wasn't his fault. He had acted on wrong information. Saracoglu— No, the governor was a civilian who was, at most, peripherally involved in fact-gathering and had worked conscientiously to help prepare. Naval Intelligence itself—but Saracoglu had spoken sooth. Real espionage against Ythri was impossible. Besides, Intelligence ... the whole navy, the whole Empire ... was spread too thin across a reach too vast, inhuman, hostile; in the end, perhaps all striving to keep the Peace of Man was barren.

You did what you could. Cajal realized he had not done badly. These events should not be called a debacle, simply a disappointment. Thanks to discipline and leadership, his fleet had taken far fewer losses than it might have; it remained overwhelmingly powerful; he had learned lessons that he would use later on in the war.

Nevertheless the ghosts would not go away.

Cajal knelt. *Christ, who forgave the soldiers, help me forgive myself. Saints, stand by me till my work is done.* His look went from crucifix to picture. *Before everyone, you, Elena who in Heaven must love me yet, since none were ever too lowly for your love, Elena, watch over me. Hold my hand.*

Beneath the flyers, the Middle Ocean rolled luminous black. Above them were stars and a Milky Way whose frostiness cut through the air's warmth. Ahead rose the thundercloud mass of an island. Tabitha heard surf on its beaches, a drumfire in the murmur across her face.

"Are they sure the thing landed here?" asked one of the half-dozen Ythrians who followed her and Draun.

"Either here or in the sea," growled her partner. "What's the home guard for if not to check out detector findings? Now be quiet. And wary. If that was an Imperial boat—"

"They're marooned," Tabitha finished for him. "Helpless."

"Then, why've they not called to be fetched?"

"Maybe their transmitter is ruined."

"And maybe they have a little scheme. I'd like that. We've many new-made dead this night. The more Terrans for hell-wind to blow ahead of them, the better."

"Follow your own orders and shut up," Tabitha snapped.

Sometimes she seriously considered dissolving her association with Draun. She had come to see over the years that he didn't really believe in the gods of the Old Faith, nor carry out their rites from traditionalism like most Highsky folk; no, he enjoyed those slaughterous sacrifices. And he had killed in duello more than once, on his own challenge, however much trouble he might have afterward in scraping together winner's gild for the bereaved. And while he seldom abused his slaves, he kept some, which she felt was the fundamental abuse.

Still—he was loyal and, in his arrogant way, generous to friends; his seamanship combined superbly with her managerial talents; he could be good company when he chose; his wife was sweet; his youngest cubs were irresistible, and loved their Kin-She Hrill who took them in her arms. . . .

*I'm perfect? Not by a fertilizing long shot, considering how I let my mind meander!*

They winged, she thrust above the strand and high over the island. Photoamplifier goggles showed it silver-gray, here and there speckled with taller growth; on boulders, dew had begun to catch starlight. (*How goes it yonder? The news said the enemy's been thrown back, but—*) She wished she were flying nude in this stroking, giddily perfumed air. But her business demanded coveralls, cuirass, helmet, boots. That which had been detected coming down might be a crippled Avalonian, but might equally well be—*Hoy!*

"Look." She pointed. "A fresh track." They swung about, crossed a ridge, and the wreck lay under them.

"Terran indeed," Draun said. She saw his crest and tail-feathers quiver in eagerness. He wheeled, holding a magnifier to his eyes. "Two outside. Hya-a-a-a-ah!"

"Stop!" Tabitha yelled, but he was already stooping.

She cursed the awkwardness of gravbelts, set controls and flung herself after him. Behind came the other Ythrians, blasters clutched to breasts while wings hastened their bodies. Draun had left his gun sheathed, had taken out instead the half-meter-long, heavy, crooked Fao knife.

"Stop!" Tabitha screamed into the whistle of split air. "Give them a chance to surrender!"

The humans, standing by a patch of freshly turned earth, heard. Their glances lifted. Draun howled his battle cry. One man yanked at a holstered sidearm. Then the hurricane was on him. Wings snapped around so it roared in the pinions. Two meters from ground, Draun turned his fall into an upward rush. His right arm swept the blade in a short arc; his left hand, on the back of it, urged it along. The Terran's head flew off the neck, hit the susin and horribly bounced. The body stood an instant, geysering blood, before it collapsed like a puppet on which the strings have been slashed.

"Hya-a-a-a-ah!" Draun shrieked. "Hell-winds blow you before my chothmates! Tell Illarian they are coming!"

The other Terran stumbled back. His own sidearm was out. He fired, a flash and boom in blackness.

*Before they kill him too*— Tabitha had no time for planning. She was in the van of her squad. The man's crazed gaze and snap shot were aimed at Draun, whose broad-winged shadow had not yet come about for a second pass. She dived from the rear, tackled him low, and rolled over, gripping fast. They tumbled; the belt wasn't able to lift both of them. She felt her brow slammed against a root, her cheek dragged abradingly over the susin.

His threshings stopped. She turned off her unit and crouched beside him. Pain and dizziness and the laboring of her lungs were remote. He wasn't dead, she saw, merely half stunned from his temple striking a rock. Blood oozed in the kinky black hair, but he stirred and his eyeballs were filled with starlight. He was tall, swarthy by Avalonian measure . . . people with such chromosomes generally settled beneath stronger suns than Laura. . . .

The Ythrians swooped near. Wind rushed in their quills. Tabitha scrambled to her feet. She bestrode the Terran. Gun in hand, she gasped, "No. Hold back. No more killing. He's mine."

# X

FERUNE of Mistwood reported in at Gray, arranged his affairs and said his goodbyes within a few days.

To Daniel Holm: "Luck be your friend, First Marchwarden."

The man's mouth was stretched and unsteady. "You must have more time than—than—"

Ferune shook his head. The crest drooped ragged; most feathers that remained to him were lusterless white; he spoke in a mutter. His grin had not changed. "No, I'm afraid the medics can't stimulate regeneration in this case. Not when every last cell got blasted. Pity the Imperials didn't try shooting us full of mercury vapor. But you'd find that inconvenient."

*Yes, you've more tolerance for heavy metals than*

115

*humans do,* went uselessly through Holm, *but less for
hard radiation.* The voice trudged on: "As is, I am
held together by drugs and baling wire. Most of those
who were with me are already dead, I hear. But I had
to get my powers and knowledge transferred to you,
didn't I, before I rest?"

"To me?" the man suddenly couldn't hold back.
"Me who killed you?"

Ferune stiffened. "Come off that perch, Daniel
Holm. If I thought you really blame yourself, I would
not have left you in office—probably not alive; anyone
that stupid would be dangerous. You were executing
my plan, and bloody-gut well it worked too, kh'hng?"

Holm knelt and laid his head on the keelbone. It
was sharp, when flesh had melted from above, and the
skin was fever-hot and he could feel how the heart
stammered. Ferune shifted to handstance. Wings
enfolded the man and lips kissed him. "I flew higher
because of you," Ferune said. "If war allows, honor
us by coming to my rite. Fair winds forever."

He left. An adjutant helped him into a car and took
him northward, to the woodlands of his choth and to
Wharr who awaited him.


"Permit me to introduce myself. I am Juan de Jesús
Cajal y Palomares of Nuevo México, commanding His
Imperial Majesty's naval forces in the present campaign. You have my word as a Terran officer that the
beam is tight, the relays are automatic, this conversation will be recorded but not monitored, and the tape
will be classified secret."

The two who looked out of the screens were silent,
until Cajal grew overaware of the metal which enclosed
him, background pulse of machinery and slight chemi-
cal taint in the air blown from ventilators. He wondered what impression he was making on them. There
was no way to tell from the old Ythrian—Liaw? Yes,
Liaw—who evidently represented civil authority. That

being sat like a statue of grimness, except for the smoldering yellow eyes. Daniel Holm kept moving, cigar in and out of his mouth, fingers drumming desktop, tic in the left cheek. He was haggard, unkempt, stubbly, grimy, no hint of Imperial neatness about him. But he scarcely seemed humble.

He it was who asked at length: "Why?"

"¿Por qué?" responded Cajal in surprise. "Why I had a signal shot down to you proposing a conference? To discuss terms, of course."

"No, this secrecy. Not that I believe you about it, or anything else."

Cajal felt his cheeks redden. *I must not grow angry.* "As you wish, Admiral Holm. However, please credit me with some common sense. Quite apart from the morality of letting the slaughter and waste of wealth proceed, you must see that I would prefer to avoid further losses. That is why we're orbiting Avalon and Morgana at a distance and have made no aggressive move since battle tapered off last week. Now that we've evaluated our options, I am ready to talk; and I hope you've likewise done some hard thinking. I am not interested in pomp or publicity. Such things only get in the way of reaching practical solutions. Therefore the confidential nature of our parley. I hope you'll take the chance to speak as frankly as I mean to, knowing your words need not commit you."

"Our word does," Holm said.

"Please," Cajal urged. "You're angry, you'd kill me were you able, nevertheless you're a fellow professional. We both have our duties, however distasteful certain of them may be."

"Well, get on with it, then. What d'you want?"

"To discuss terms, I said. I realize we three alone can't authorize or arrange the surrender, but—"

"I think you can," Liaw interrupted: a low, dry, harshly accented Anglic. "If you fear court-martial afterward, we will grant you asylum."

Cajal's mouth fell open. "What are you saying?"

"We must be sure this is no ruse. I suggest you bring your ships one at a time into close orbit, for boarding. Transportation home for the crews will be made available later."

"Do you ... do you—" Cajal swallowed. "Sir, I'm told your proper title translates more or less into 'Judge' or 'Lawspeaker.' Judge, this is no time for humor."

"If you don't want to give in," Holm said, "what's to discuss?"

"Your capitulation, *por Díos!*" Cajal's fist smote the arm of his chair. "I'm not going to play word games. You've delayed us too long already. But your fleet has been smashed. Its fragments are scattered. A minor detachment from our force can hunt them down at leisure. We control all space around you. You've no possibility of outside help. Whatever might recklessly be sent from other systems would be annihilated in detail; and the admiralties there know it. If they go anywhere with what pitiful strength they have, it'll be to Quetlan." He leaned forward. "We'd hate to bombard your planet. Please don't compel us to."

"Go right ahead," Holm answered. "Our interceptor crews would enjoy the practice."

"But—are you expecting blockade runners to—to— Oh, I know how big a planet is. I know an occasional small craft could sneak past our detector grids, our patrols and stations. But I also know how very small such craft must be, and how very occasional their success."

Holm drew savagely on his cigar before he stabbed it into its smoke. "Yes, sure," he snapped. "Standard technique. Eliminate a space fleet, and its planet has to yield or you'll pound it into radioactive slag. Nice work for a man, that, hunh? Well, my colleagues and I saw this war coming years back. We knew we'd never have much of a navy by comparison, if only because you bastards have so much more population and area behind you. But defense— Admiral, you're at the end of a long line of communication and supply. The border worlds aren't geared to produce anything like the amount of stuff you require; it has to come from deeper in the Empire. We're *here*, set up to make everything necessary as fast as necessary. We can't come after you. But we can bugger well swamp whatever you throw at us."

"Absolutely?"

"Okay, once in a great while, by sheer luck, you doubtless could land a warhead, and it might be big and dirty. We'd weather that, and the home guard has decontamination teams. Chances of its hitting anything important are about like drawing three for a royal flush. No ship of yours can get close enough with an energy projector husky enough to pinken a baby's bottom. But there're no size and mass limits on our ground-based photon weapons; we can use whole rivers to cool their generators while their snouts whiff you out of our sky. Now tell me why in flaming chaos we should surrender."

Cajal sat back. He felt as if struck from behind.

"No harm in learning what conditions you meant to offer," Liaw said, toneless.

*Face saving? Those Ythrians are supposed to be satanically proud, but not to the point of lunacy.* Hope knocked in Cajal. "Honorable terms, of course," he said. "Your ships must be sequestered, but they will not be used against Ythri and personnel may go home, officers to keep their sidearms. Likewise for your defensive facilities. You must accept occupation and cooperate with the military government, but every effort will be made to respect your laws and customs, individuals will have the right to petition for redress of grievances, and Terran violators of the statutes will be punished as severely as Avalonian. Actually, if the population behaves correctly, I doubt if a large percentage will ever even see an Imperial marine."

"And after the war?"

"Why, that's for the Crown to decide, but I presume you'll be included in a reorganized Sector Pacis, and you must know Governor Saracoglu is efficient and humane. Insofar as possible, the Empire allows home rule and the continuation of local ways of life."

"Allows. The operative word. But let it pass. Let us assume a degree of democracy. Could we stop immigrants from coming until they outvoted us?"

"Well . . . well, no. Citizens are guaranteed freedom of movement. That's one of the things the Empire is for. Confound it, you can't selfishly block progress just because you prefer archaism."

"There is no more to discuss. Good day, Admiral."

"No, wait! Wait! You can't—condemn your whole people to war by yourselves!"

"If the Khruaths and the Parliament change their views, you will be informed."

"But listen, you're letting them die for nothing," Cajal said frantically. "This frontier is going to be straightened out. You, the whole Domain of Ythri have no power to stop that. You can only prolong the murderous, maiming farce. And you'll be punished by worse peace terms than you could have had. Listen, it's not one-sided. You're coming into the Empire. You'll get trade, contact, protection. Cooperate now and I swear you'll start out as a chartered client state, with all the privileges that means. Within years, individuals will be getting Terran citizenship. Eventually the whole of Avalon could become part of Greater Terra. For the love of God, be realistic!"

"We are," said Liaw.

Holm leered. Both screens blanked.

Cajal sat for minutes, staring. *They can't have been serious. They can't.* Twice he reached toward his intercom.

Have them called; maybe this was some childish insistence that the Empire beg them to negotiate. . . .

His hand drew back. *No. I am responsible for our own dignity.*

Decision came. Let Plan Two be set in train. Leave the calculated strength here to invest Avalon. Comparatively little would be required. The sole real purpose was to keep this world's considerable resources from flowing to Ythri and these bases from menacing Cajal's lines back to the Empire. Siege would tie up more men and vessels than occupation would have done, but he could spare them.

The important thing was not to lose momentum. Rather, his freed ships must be off immediately to help in simultaneous assaults on Khrau and Hru. He'd direct the former himself, his second in command the latter. What they had learned here would be quite helpful.

And he was sure of quick victories yonder. Intelligence had failed to learn the extent of Avalonian arming, but not to discover the fact itself; that could not be concealed. By the same token, he knew that no other planet of the Domain had had a Daniel Holm nagging it over the years to build against this storm. He knew that the other Ythrian colonial fleets were small and poorly coordinated, the worlds unarmed.

Quetlan, the home sun, was more formidable. But let him rip spectacularly enough through the spaces between, and he dared hope his enemies would have the wisdom to capitulate before he stabbed them in the heart.

*And afterward a few distorted molecules, recording the armistice, will give us Avalon. Very well. Better than fighting. . . . Do they know this? Do they merely want to keep, for a few weeks more, the illusion of freedom? Well, I hope the price they'll be charged for that—levies, restrictions, revisions of their whole society, that might otherwise have been deemed*

*unnecessary—I hope they won't find the price unen-
durably steep—because endure it they must.*

Before sunrise, Ferune departed Mistwood.

That day his home country bore its name well. Fog
blew cold, wet, and blinding off the sea. Smokiness
prowled the glooms around thick boles of hammerbranch, soaring trunks of lightningrod; moisture
dripped from boughs onto fallen leaves, and where it
struck a pool which had formed among the ringed
stems of a sword-of-sorrow, it made a tiny glass chim-
ing. But deeper inland, where Old Avalon remained,
a boomer tree frightened beasts that might have
grazed on it, and this noise rolled beneath the house
of Ferune and echoed off the hanging shields of his
ancestors.

Wings gathered. A trumpet sounded through night.
Forth came his sons to meet their chothmates. They
carried the body on a litter between them. His uhoths
fluttered about, puzzled at his quietness. His widow
led the way. Flanking were his daughters, their husbands and grown children, who bore lit torches.

Wings beat. The flight cut upward. When it rose
past the fog, this was turned to blue-shadowed white
under an ice-pale eastern lightening. Westward over
sea, the last stars glimmered in royal purple.

Still the folk mounted, until they were near the top
of what unaided flesh could reach. Here the airs whit-
tered thin and chill; but on the rim of a twilit world,
the snowpeaks of the Weathermother were kindled by
a yet hidden sun.

All this while the flight beat north. Daniel Holm and
his family, following in heavy garments and breathing
masks, saw wings glow across heaven in one tremendous spearhead. They could barely make out the
torchflames which streamed at its point, as sparks like
the waning stars. More clearly came the throb from
under those pinions. Apart from that, silence was total.

They reached wilderness, a land of crags, boulders, and swift-running streams. There the sons of Ferune stopped. Wings outspread, they hovered on the first faint warmth of morning, their mother before them. Around circled their near kin; and in a wheel, the choth surrounded these. And the sun broke over the mountains.

To Ferune came the new Wyvan of Mistwood. Once more he blew the horn, and thrice he called the name of the dead. Wharr swept by, to kiss farewell. Then the Wyvan spoke the words of the New Faith, which was two thousand years old.

"High flew your spirit on many winds; but downward upon you at last came winging God the Hunter. You met Him in pride, you fought Him well, from you He has honor. Go hence now, that which the talons left, be water and leaves, arise in the wind; and spirit, be always remembered."

His sons tilted the litter. The body fell, and after it the torches.

Wharr slanted off in the beginning measures of the sky dance. A hundred followed her.

Hanging afar, between emptiness and immensity, Daniel Holm said to Christopher: "And that Terran thought we'd surrender."

# XI

LIAW of The Tarns spoke. "We are met in the Great Khruath of Avalon, that free folk may choose their way. Our enemy has taken elsewhere most of the might which he brought against us. This is no victory, since those vessels will make war upon the rest of the Domain. Meanwhile he has left sufficient ships to hold us cut off. They are unlikely to attack our world. But they will seek to find and root out our bases among the sister planets and the few warcraft of ours that are left in space. Save for what harassment our brethren aboard can contrive, we have no means of taking the offensive. Our defenses we can maintain indefinitely. Yet no pledge can be given that great harm will not be wrought on Avalon, should the foe launch a determined effort. He has declared that in the end we are sure to be subjugated. This is possibly true. He has then declared that we can expect better treatment if we yield now than if we fight on, though at best we will come under Imperial law and custom. This is certainly true.

"They who speak for you rejected the demand, as was their duty until you could be summoned to decide. I remind you of the hazards of continued war and the threat of a harsh peace should we lose. I remind you furthermore that if we do resist, the free folk of Avalon must give up many of their rights and submit to the dictation of military leaders for as long as the strife may last.

"What say the choths?"

He and his colleagues stood on the olden site, First Island in the Hesperian Sea. At their backs rose the house of David Falkayn; before them greensward slanted toward beach and surf. But no booths or tents had been raised, no ships lay at anchor, no swarms of delegates flew down to form ranks beneath the trees. Time was lacking for ceremonious assemblies. Those elected at regional meetings, and those individuals who signified a wish to speak, were present electronically.

A computer-equipped staff worked hard inside the house. However taciturn the average Ythrian was, however unwilling to make a fool of himself by declaiming the obvious, still, when some two million enfranchised adults were hooked into a matter of as great moment as this, the questions and comments that arrived must be filtered. Those chosen to be heard must wait their turns.

Arinnian knew he would be called. He sat by Eyath before an outsize screen. They were alone on the front, hence lowest bench. At their backs the tiers rose, the household of Lythran and Blawsa crowded thereon, to the seat of the master and his lady. Liaw's slow words only deepened the quiet in that broad, dark, weaponhung chamber; and so did the rustle of feathers, the scrape of claws or alatans, when someone shifted a little. The air was filled with the woodsmoke odor of Ythrian bodies. A breeze, gusting in from a window open on rain, added smells of damp earth and stirred the banners that hung from high rafters.

"—report on facts concerning—"

The image in the screen became that of a rancher. Behind him could be seen the North Coronan prairie, a distant herd, a string of quadrupedal burden-bearing zirraukhs led by a flapping youth, a more up-to-date truck which passed overhead. He stated, "Food production throughout the Plains of Long Reach has been satisfactory this year. The forecasts for next season are optimistic. We have achieved 75 percent storage of preserved meat in bunkers proofed against radioactive contamination, and expect to complete this task by midwinter. Details are filed in Library Central. Finished." The scan returned to the High Wyvans, who promptly called on another area representative.

Eyath caught Arinnian's arm. He felt the pulse in her fingers, and the claws on the two encircling thumbs bit him. He looked at her. The bronze-brown crest was stiffly raised, the amber eyes like lanterns. Fangs gleamed between her lips. "Must they drone on till eternity molders?" she breathed.

"They need truth before they decide," he whispered back, and felt the disapproving stares between his shoulderblades.

"What's to decide—when Vodan's in space?"

"You help him best by patience." He wondered who he was to give counsel. Well, Eyath was young (*me too, but this day I feel old*) and it was cruel that she could hope for no word of her betrothed until, probably, war's end. No mothership could venture in beaming range of beleaguered Avalon.

At least it was known that Vodan's had been among those which escaped. Too many orbited in wreck.

More Terrans had been destroyed, of course, thanks to the trap that Ferune and Holm sprang. But one Ythrian slain was too many, Arinnian thought, and a million Terrans were too few.

"—call on the chief of the West Coronan guard."

He scrambled to his feet, realized that was unnecessary, and opined that he'd better remain standing than compound his gaucherie by sitting down again before he had spoken. "Uh, Arinnian of Stormgate. We're in good shape, equipping, training, and assigning recruits as fast as they come in. But we want more. Uh, since nobody has mentioned it, I'd like to remind people that except for ranking officers, home-guard service is part-time and the volunteer's schedule can be set to minimize interference with his ordinary work. Our section's cooperation with the North Oronesians is now being extended through the entire archipelago, and we aim to do likewise in southerly and easterly directions till, uh, we've an integrated command for the Brendan's, Fiery, and Shielding Islands as well, to protect the whole perimeter of Corona.

"Uh, on behalf of my father, the First Marchwarden, I want to point out a considerable hole in Avalon's defense, namely the absence of a guard for Equatoria, nothing there except some projector and missile launching sites. True, the continent's uninhabited, but the Terrans know that, and if they consider an invasion, they aren't likely to care about preserving a piece of native ecology intact. I, uh, will receive suggestions about this and pass them along the proper channels." His tongue was dry. "Finished."

He lowered himself. Eyath took his hand, gentler this time. Thank fortune, no one wanted to question him. He could be crisp in discussing strictly technical problems with a few knowledgeable persons, but two million were a bit much for a man without political instincts.

The talk seemed interminable. And yet, at the end,

when the vote was called, when Liaw made his matter-of-fact announcement that the data bank recorded 83 percent in favor of continued resistance, scarcely six hours had passed. Humans couldn't have done it.

"Well," Arinnian said into the noise of cramped wings being stretched, "no surprises."

Eyath tugged at him. "Come," she said. "Get your belt. I want to use my muscles before dinner."

Rain beat through dusk, cold and tasting of sky. When they came above the clouds, he and she turned east to get away from their chothmates who also sought exercise. Snowpeaks and glaciers thrust out of whiteness, into a blue-black where gleamed the early stars and a few moving sparks which were orbital fortresses.

They fared awhile in silence, until she said: "I'd like to join the guard."

"Hm? Ah. Yes; welcome."

"But not fly patrol. That's essential, I know, and pleasant if the weather's halfway good; but I don't want a lot of pleasure. Look, see Camelot rising yonder. Vodan may be huddled inside a dead moon of it, waiting and waiting for a chance to hazard his life."

"What would you prefer?" he asked.

Her wings beat more steadily than her voice. "You must be caught in a hurricane of work, which is bound to stiffen. Surely your staff's too small, else why would you be so tired? Can't I help?"

"M-m . . . well—"

"Your assistant, your fetch-and-carry lass, even your personal secretary? I can take an electro-cram in the knowledge and skills, and be ready to start inside a few days."

"No. That's rough."

"I'll survive. Try me. Fire me if I can't grip the task, and we'll stay friends. I believe I can, though. Maybe better than someone who hasn't known you all these years, and who can be given another job. I'm bright and energetic. Am I not? And ... Arinnian, I so much need to be with you, till this cripplewing time is outlived."

She reached toward him. He caught her hand. "Very well, galemate." In the wan light she flew as beautiful as ever beneath sun or moon.

"Yes, I'll call for a vote tomorrow," Matthew Vickery said.

"How d'you expect it'll go?" Daniel Holm asked.

The President sighed. "How do you think? Oh, the war faction won't bring in quite the majority of Parliament that it did of the Khruath. A few members will vote their convictions rather than their mail. But I've seen the analysis of that mail, and of the phone calls and— Yes, you'll get your damned resolution to carry on. You'll get your emergency powers, the virtual suspension of civilian government you've been demanding. I do wish you'd read some of those letters or watch some of those tapes. The fanaticism might frighten you as it does me. I never imagined we had that much latent insanity in our midst."

"It's insane to fight for your home?"

Vickery bit his lip. "Yes, when nothing can be gained."

"I'd say we gain quite a chunk. We kicked a sizable hole in the Terran armada. We're tying up a still bigger part, that was originally supposed to be off to Ythri."

"Do you actually believe the Domain can beat the Empire? Holm, the Empire can't *afford* to compromise. Take its viewpoint for a minute if you can. The solitary keeper of the peace among thousands of wildly diverse peoples; the solitary guardian of the borders against the barbarian and the civilized predatory alien, who carry nuclear weapons. The Empire has to be more than almighty. It must maintain credibility,

universal belief that it's irresistible, or hell's kettle
boils over."

"My nose bleeds for the Empire," Holm said, "but
His Majesty will have to solve his problems at somebody else's expense. He gets no free rides from us.
Besides, you'll note the Terrans didn't keep throwing
themselves at Avalon."

"They had no need to," Vickery replied. "If the
need does arise, they'll be back in force. Meanwhile
we're contained." He filled his lungs. "I admit your
gamble paid off extraordinarily—"

"Please. 'Investment.' And not mine. Ours."

"But don't you see, now there's nothing further we
can use it for except a bargaining counter? We can
get excellent terms, and I've dealt with Governor Saracoglu, I know he'll see to it that agreements are honored. Rationally considered, what's so dreadful about
coming under the Empire?"

"Well, we'd begin by breaking our oath to Ythri.
Sorry, chum. Deathpride doesn't allow."

"You sit here mouthing obsolete words, but I tell
you, the winds of change are blowing."

"I understand that's a mighty old phrase too," Holm
said. "Ferune had one still older that he liked to
quote. How'd it go? '—their finest hour—'"

Tabitha Falkayn shoved off from the dock and
hauled on two lines in quick succession. Jib and main-
sail crackled, caught the breeze, and bellied taut. The
light, open boat heeled till foam hissed along the star-
board rail, and accelerated outward. Once past the
breakwater, on open sea, she began to ride waves.

"We're planing!" Philippe Rochefort cried.

"Of course," Tabitha answered. "This is a hydrofoil.
'Ware boom." She put the helm down. The yard
swung, the hull skipped onto the other tack.

"No keel? What do you do for lateral resistance?"

She gestured at the oddly curved boards which

lifted above either rail, pivoting in response to vanes
upon them. "Those. The design's Ythrian. They know
more about the ways of wind than men and men's
computers can imagine."

Rochefort settled down to admire the view. It was
superb. Billows marched as far as he could see, blue
streaked with violet and green, strewn with sun-glitter,
intricately white-foamed. They rumbled and whooshed.
Fine spindrift blew off them, salty on the lips, spurring
the blood where it struck bare skin. The air was cool,
not cold, and singingly alive. Aft, the emerald heights
of St. Li dwindled at an astonishing speed.

He had to admit the best part was the big, tawny
girl who stood, pipe in teeth, hawklike pet on shoulder, bleached locks flying, at the tiller. She wore nothing but a kilt, which the wind molded to her loins,
and—to be sure—her knife and blaster.

"How far did you say?" he asked.

" 'Bout thirty-five kilometers. A couple of hours at
this rate. We needn't start back till sundown, plenty
of starlight to steer by, so you'll have time for poking
around."

"You're too kind, Donna," he said carefully.

She laughed. "No, I'm grateful for an excuse to take
an outing. Especially since those patches of atlantis
weed fascinate me. Entire ecologies, in areas that may
get bigger'n the average island. And the fisher scout
told me he'd seen a kraken grazing the fringes of this
one. Hope we find him. They're a rare sight. Peaceful,
though we dare not come too near something that
huge."

"I meant more than this excursion," Rochefort said.
"You receive me, a prisoner of war, as your house
guest."

Tabitha shrugged. "Why not? We don't bother
stockading what few people we've taken. They aren't
going anywhere." Her eyes rested candidly on him.
"Besides, I want to know you."

He wondered, with an inward thump, how well.

Somberness crossed her. "And," she said, "I hope to . . . make up for what happened. You've got to see that Draun didn't wantonly murder your friend. He's, well, impetuous; and a gun was being pulled; and it *is* wartime."

He ventured a smile. "Won't always be, Donna."

"Tabitha's the name, Philippe; or Hrill when I talk Planha. You don't, of course. . . . That's right. When you go home, I'd like you to realize we Ythrians aren't monsters."

"Ythrians? You?" He raised his brows.

"What else? Avalon belongs to the Domain."

"It won't for much longer," Rochefort said. In haste: "Against that day, I'll do what I can to show you we Terrans aren't monsters either."

He could not understand how she was able to grin so lightheartedly. "If it amuses you to think that, you're welcome. I'm afraid you'll find amusement in rather short supply here. Swimming, fishing, boating, hiking . . . and, yes, reading; I'm addicted to mystery stories and have a hefty stack, some straight from Terra. But that's just about the list. I'm the sole human permanently resident on St. Li, and between them, my business and my duties as a home-guard officer will keep me away a lot."

"I'll manage," he said.

"Sure, for a while," she replied. "The true Ythrians aren't hostile to you. They mostly look on war as an impersonal thing, like a famine where you might have to kill somebody to feed him to your young but don't hate him on that account. They don't go in for chitchat, but if you play chess you'll find several opponents."

Tabitha shortened the mainsheet and left it in a snap cleat. "Still," she said, "Avalonians of either kind don't mass-produce entertainment, the way I hear people do in the Empire. You won't find much on the screens except news, sleepifyingly earnest educational

programs, and classic dramas which probably won't
mean a thing to you. So . . . when you get bored, tell
me and I'll arrange for your quartering in a town like
Gray or Centauri."

"I don't expect to be," he said, and added in measured softness, "Tabitha." Nonetheless he spoke hon-
estly when he shook his head, stared over the waters,
and continued: "No, I feel guilty at not grieving more,
at being as conscious as I am of my fantastic good
luck."

"Ha!" she chuckled. "Someday I'll count up the different ways you were lucky. That was an unconverted
island you were on, lad, pure Old Avalonian, including
a fair sample of the nastier species."

"Need an armed man, who stays alert, fear any animals here?"

"Well, no doubt you could shoot a spathodont dead
before it fanged you, though reptiloids don't kill easy.
I wouldn't give odds on you against a pack of lycosauroids, however; and if a kakkelak swarm started running
up your trousers—" Tabitha grimaced. "But those're
tropical mainland beasties. You'd have had your troubles from the plants, which're wider distributed. Suppose a gust stirred the limbs of a surgeon tree as you
walked by. Or . . . right across the ridge from where
you were, I noticed a hollow full of hell shrub. You're
no Ythrian, to breathe those vapors and live."

"Brrr!" he said. "What incurable romantic named
this planet?"

"David Falkayn's granddaughter, when he'd decided
this was the place to go," she answered, grave again.
"And they were right, both of them. If anything, the
problem was to give native life its chance. Like the
centaurs, who're a main reason for declaring Equatoria
off limits, because they use bits of stone and bone in
tool fashion and maybe in a million years they could
become intelligent. And by the way, their protection

was something Ythri insisted on, hunter Ythri, not the human pioneers."

She gestured. "Look around you," she said. "This is our world. It's going to stay ours."

*No*, he thought, and the day was dulled for him, *you're wrong, Tabitha-Hrill. My admiral is going to hammer your Ythrians until they have no choice but to hand you over to my Emperor.*

# XII

WEEK after fire-filled week, the Terran armada advanced.

Cajal realized that despite its inauspicious start, his campaign would become a textbook classic. In fact, his decision about Avalon typified it. Any fool could smash through with power like his. As predicted, no other colonial system possessed armament remotely comparable to what he had encountered around Laura. What existed was handled with acceptable skill, but simply had no possibility of winning.

So any butcher could have spent lives and ships, and milled his opposition to dust in the course of months. Intelligence data and Cajal's own estimate had shown that this was the approach his enemies expected him to take. They in their turn would fight delaying actions, send raiders into the Empire, seek to stir up third parties such as Merseia, and in general make the war sufficiently costly for Terra that a negotiated peace would become preferable.

Cajal doubted this would work, even under the most favorable circumstances. He knew the men who sat on the Policy Board. Nevertheless he felt his duty was to avoid victory by attrition—his duty to both realms. Thus he had planned, not a cautious advance where every gain was consolidated before the next was made, but a swordstroke.

Khrau and Hru fell within days of the Terrans' crossing their outermost planetary orbits. Cajal left a few ships in either system and a few occupation troops, mostly technicians, on the habitable worlds.

These forces looked ludicrously small. Marchwarden Rusa collected a superior one and sought to recapture Khrau. The Terrans sent word and hung on. A detachment of the main fleet came back, bewilderingly soon, and annihilated Rusa's command.

On Hru III the choths rose in revolt. They massacred part of the garrison. Then the missiles struck from space. Not many were needed before the siege of the Imperials was called off. The Wyvans were rounded up and shot. This was done with proper respect for their dignity. Some of them, in final statements, urged their people to cooperate with relief teams being rushed from Esperance to the smitten areas.

Meanwhile the invaders advanced on Quetlan. From their main body, tentacles reached out to grab system after system in passing. Most of these Cajal did not bother to occupy. He was content to shatter their navies and go on. After six weeks, the sun of Ythri was englobed by lost positions.

Now the armada was deep into the Domain, more than 50 light-years from the nearest old-established Imperial base. The ornithoids would never have a better chance of cutting it off. If they gathered everything they had for a decisive combat—not a standup slugging match, of course; a running fight that might last weeks—they would still be somewhat outmatched in numbers. But they would have a continuing supply of munitions, which the Imperials would not.

Cajal gave them every opportunity. They obliged.

The Battle of Yarro Cluster took eight standard days, from the first engagement to the escape of the last lonely Ythrian survivors. But the first two of these days were preliminary and the final three were scarcely more than a mopping up. Details are for the texts. In essence, Cajal made use of two basic advantages. The first was surprise; he had taken pains to keep secret the large number of ammunition carriers with him. The second was organization; he could play his fleet like an instrument, luring and jockeying the ill-coordinated enemy units into death after death.

Perhaps he also possessed a third advantage, genius. When that thought crossed his mind, he set himself a penance.

The remnants of Domain power reeled back toward Quetlan. Cajal followed leisurely.

Ythri was somewhat smaller than Avalon, somewhat drier, the cloud cover more thin and hence the land masses showing more clearly from space, tawny and rusty in hue, under the light of a sun more cool and yellow than Laura. Yet it was very lovely, floating among the stars. Cajal left that viewscreen on and from time to time glanced thither, away from the face in his comboard.

The High Wyvan Trauvay said, "You are bold to enter our home." His Anglic was fluent, and he employed a vocalizer for total clarity of pronunciation.

Cajal met the unblinking yellow eyes and answered, "You agreed to a parley. I trust your honor." *I put faith in my Supernova and her escort, too. Better remind him.* "This war is a sorrow to me. I would hate to blacken any part of your world or take any further lives of your gallant folk."

"That might not be simple to do, Admiral," Trauvay said slowly. "We have defenses."

"Observed. Wyvan, may I employ blunt speech?"

"Yes. Particularly since this is, you understand, not a binding discussion."

*No, but half a billion Ythrians are tuned in,* Cajal thought. *I wish they weren't. It's as if I could feel them.*

*What kind of government is this? Not exactly democratic—you can't hang any Terran label on it, not even "government," really. Might we humans have something to learn here? Everything we try seems to break down at last, and the only answer to that which we ever seem to find is the brute simplicity of Caesar.*

*Stop, Juan! You're an officer of the Imperium.*

"I thank the Wyvan," Cajal said, "and request him and his people to believe we will not attack them further unless forced or ordered to do so. At present we have no reason for it. Our objectives have been achieved. We can now make good our rightful claims along the border. Any resistance must be sporadic and, if you will pardon the word, pathetic. A comparatively minor force can blockade Quetlan. Yes, naturally individual ships can steal past now and then. But to all intents and purposes, you will be isolated from your extrasystemic possessions, allies, and associates. Please consider how long the Domain can survive as a political entity under such conditions.

"Please consider, likewise, how your holding out will be an endless expense, an endless irritation to the Imperium. Sooner or later, it will decide to eliminate the nuisance. I do not say this is just, I say merely it is true. I myself would appeal an order to open fire. Were it too draconian, I would resign. But His Majesty has many admirals."

Stillness murmured around crucified Christ. Finally Trauvay asked, "Do you call for our surrender?"

"For an armistice," Cajai said.

"On what conditions?"

"A mutual cease-fire, of course ... by definition! Captured ships and other military facilities will be retained by Terra, but prisoners will be repatriated on both sides. We will remain in occupation of systems we have entered, and will occupy those worlds claimed by the Imperium which have not already been taken. Local authorities and populaces will submit to the military officers stationed among them. For our part, we pledge respect for law and custom, rights of nonseditious free speech and petition, interim economic assistance, resumption of normal trade as soon as possible, and the freedom of any individual who so desires to sell his property on the open market and leave. Certain units of this fleet will stay near Quetlan and frequently pass through the system on surveillance; but they will not land unless invited, nor interfere with commerce, except that they reserve the right of inspection to verify that no troops or munitions are being sent."

Waves passed over the feathers. Cajal wished he knew how to read them. The tone stayed flat: "You do demand surrender."

The man shook his head. "No, sir, I do not, and in fact that would exceed my orders. The eventual terms of peace are a matter for diplomacy."

"What hope have we if defeat be admitted beforehand?"

"Much." Cajal made ready his lungs. "I respectfully suggest you consult your students of human sociodynamics. To put it crudely, you have two influences to exert, one negative, one positive. The negative one is your potentiality of renewing the fight. Recall that most of your industry remains intact in your hands, that you have ships left which are bravely and ably manned, and that your home star is heavily defended and would cost us dearly to reduce.

"Wyvan, people of Ythri, I give you my most solemn assurance the Empire does not want to overrun you. Why should we take on the burden? Worse than the direct expense and danger would be the loss of a high civilization. We desire, we need your friendship. If anything, this war has been fought to remove certain causes of friction. Now let us go on together.

"True, I cannot predict the form of the eventual peace treaty. But I call your attention to numerous public statements by the Imperium. They are quite explicit. And they are quite sincere, for it is obviously to the best interest of the Imperium that its word be kept credible.

"The Domain must yield various territories. But compensations can be agreed on. And, after all, everywhere that your borders do not march with ours, there is waiting for you a whole universe."

Cajal prayed he was reciting well. His speeches had been composed by specialists, and he had spent hours in rehearsal. But if the experts had misjudged or he had bungled—

*O God, let the slaughter end . . . and forgive me that the back of my mind is fascinated by the technical problem of capturing that planet.*

Trauvay sat moveless for minutes before he said, "This shall be considered. Please hold yourself in the vicinity for consultations." Elsewhere in the ship, a xenologist who had made Ythrians his lifetime work leaped out of his chair, laughing and weeping, to shout, "The war's over! The war's over!"

Bells rang through Fleurville, from the cathedral a great bronze striding, from lesser steeples a frolic. Rockets cataracted upward to explode softly against the stars of summer. Crowds rolled in the streets, drunk more on happiness than on any liquor; they blew horns, they shouted, and every woman was kissed by a hundred strange men who suddenly loved her. In daylight, Imperial marines paraded to trumpets and squadrons of aircraft or small spacecraft roared recklessly low. But to the capital of Esperance and Sector Pacis, joy had come by night.

High on a hill, in the conservatory of the gubernatorial palace, Ekrem Saracoglu looked out over the galaxy of the city. He knew why it surged so mightily—the noise reached him as a distant wavebeat—and shone so brilliantly. The pacifist heritage of the colonists was a partial cause; now they could stop hating those brothers who wore the Emperor's uniform. *Although,* his mind murmured, *I suspect plain animal relief speaks louder. The smell of fear has been on this planet since the first border incidents, thick since war officially began. An Ythrian raid, breaking through our surprised cordons—a sky momentarily incandescent—*

"Peace," Luisa said. "I have trouble believing."

Saracoglu glanced at the petite shape beside him. Luisa Carmen Cajal y Gómez had not dressed gaily after accepting his invitation to dinner. Her gown was correct as to length and pattern, but plain gray velvyl. Apart from a tiny gold cross between the breasts, her jewelry was a few synthetic diamonds in her hair. They glistened among high-piled black tresses like the night suns shining through the transparency overhead, or like the tears that stood on her lashes.

The governor, who had covered his portliness with lace, ruffles, tiger-patterned arcton waistcoat, green iridon culottes, snowy shimmerlyn stockings, and gems wherever he could find a place, ventured to pat her hand. "You are afraid the fighting may resume? No. Impossible. The Ythrians are not insane. By taking our armistice terms, they acknowledged defeat to themselves even more than to us. Your father should be home soon. His work is done." He sighed, trusting it wasn't too theatrically. "Mine, of course, will get rougher."

"Because of the negotiations?" she asked.

"Yes. Not that I'll have plenipotentiary status. However, I will be a ranking Terran representative, and the Imperium will rely heavily on the advice of my staff and myself. After all, this sector will continue to border on the Domain, and will incorporate the new worlds."

Her look was disconcertingly weighing from eyes that young. "You'll become quite an important man, won't you, Your Excellency?" Her tone was, if not chilly, cool.

Saracoglu got busy pinching withered petals off a fuchsia. Beside it a cinnamon bush—Ythrian plant—filled the air with fragrance. "Well, yes," he said. "I would not be false to you, Donna, including false modesty."

"The sector expanded and reorganized. You probably getting an elevation in the peerage, maybe a knighthood. At last, pretty likely, called Home and offered a Lord Advisorship."

"One is permitted to daydream."

"You promoted this war, Governor."

Saracoglu ran a palm over his bare scalp. *All right,* he decided. *If she can't see or doesn't care that it was on her account I sent Helga and Georgette packing (surely, by now, the gossip about that has reached her, though she's said no word, given no sign), well, I can probably get them back; or if they won't, there's no dearth of others. No doubt this particular daydream of mine is simply man's eternal silly refusal to admit he's growing old and fat. I've learned what the best condiments are when one must eat disappointment.*

*But how vivid she is among the flowers.*

"I promoted action to end a bad state of affairs before it got worse," he told her. "The Ythrians are no martyred saints. They advanced their interests every bit as ruthlessly as their resources allowed. Human beings were killed. Donna, my oath is to Terra."

Still her eyes dwelt on him. "Nevertheless you must have known what this would do for your career," she said, still quiet.

He nodded. "Certainly. Will you believe that that did not simplify, it vastly complicated things for me? I *thought* I thought this border rectification would be for the best. And, yes, I think I can do a better than average job, first in rebuilding out here, not least in building a reconciliation with Ythri; later, if I'm lucky, on the Policy Board, where I can instigate a number of reforms. Ought I to lay down this work in order that my conscience may feel smug? Am I wicked to enjoy the work?"

Saracoglu reached in a pocket for his cigaret case. "Perhaps the answer to those questions is yes," he finished. "How can a mortal man be sure?"

Luisa took a pair of steps in his direction. Amidst the skips of his heart he remembered to maintain his rueful half-smile. "Oh, Ekrem—" She stopped. "I'm sorry, Your Excellency."

"No, I am honored, Donna," he said.

She didn't invite him to use her given name, but she did say, smiling through tears, "I'm sorry, too, for what I hinted. I didn't mean it. I'd never have come tonight if I hadn't gotten to know you for a . . . a decent man."

"I hardly dared hope you would accept," he told her, reasonably truthfully. "You could be celebrating with people your age."

The diamonds threw scintillations when she shook her head. "No, not for something like this. Have you heard I was engaged to be married once? He was killed in action two years ago. Preventive action, it was called—putting down some tribes that had refused to follow the 'advice' of an Imperial resident— Well."

She drew breath. "Tonight I couldn't find words to thank God. Peace was too big a gift for words."

"You're the Admiral's daughter," he said. "You know peace is never a free gift."

"Do wars come undeserved?"

A discreet cough interrupted. Saracoglu turned. He was expecting his butler to announce cocktails, and the sight of a naval uniform annoyed him. "Yes?" he snapped.

"If you please, sir," the officer said nervously.

"Pray excuse me, Donna." Saracoglu bowed over Luisa's wonderfully slim hand and followed the man out into the hall.

"Well?" he demanded.

"Courier from our forces at Laura, sir." The officer shivered and was pale. "You know, that border planet Avalon."

"I do know." Saracoglu braced himself.

"Well, sir, they got word of the armistice all right. Only they reject it. They insist they'll keep on fighting."

# XIII

THE bony, bearded face in the screen said, on a note close to desperation, "Sirs, you are . . . are behaving as if you were mad."

"We've got company," Daniel Holm replied.

"Do you then propose to secede from the Domain?" Admiral Cajal exclaimed.

"No. The idea is to stay in it. We're happy there. No Imperial bureaucrats need apply."

"But the armistice agreement—"

"Sure, let's keep the present cease-fire. Avalon doesn't want to hurt anybody."

Cajal's mouth stiffened. "You cannot pick and choose among clauses. Your government has declared the Empire may occupy this system pending the final peace settlement."

Liaw of The Tarns thrust his frosty head toward the scanner that sent his image to Holm's office and Cajal's orbiting warcraft. "Ythrian practice is not Terran," he said. "The worlds of the Domain are tied to each other principally by vows of mutual fidelity. That our fellows are no longer able to help us does not give them the right to order that we cease defending ourselves. If anything, deathpride requires that we continue the fight for what help it may afford them."

Cajal lifted a fist into view. "Sirs," he rasped, "you seem to think this is the era of the Troubles and your opponents are barbarians who'll lose purpose and organization and go away if they're stalled for a while. The truth is, you're up against Imperial Terra, which thinks in terms of centuries and reigns over thousands of planets. Not that any such time or power must be spent on you. Practically the entire force that broke the Domain can now be brought to bear on your single globe. And it will be, sirs. If you compel the outcome, it will be."

His gaze smoldered upon them. "You have strong defenses," he said, "but you must understand how they can be swamped. Resistance will buy you nothing except the devastation of your homes, the death of thousands or millions. Have *they* been consulted?"

"Yes," Liaw replied. "Between the news of Ythri's capitulation and your own arrival, Khruath and Parliament voted again. A majority favors holding on."

"How big a majority this time?" Cajal asked shrewdly. He saw feathers stir and facial muscles twitch, and nodded. "I do not like the idea of making war on potentially valuable subjects of His Majesty," he said, "most especially not on women and children."

Holm swallowed. "Uh, Admiral. How about ... evacuating everybody that shouldn't stay or doesn't want to ... before we start fighting again?"

Cajal sat motionless. His features congealed. When

he spoke, it was as if his throat pained him. "No. I may not help an enemy rid himself of his liabilities."

"Are you bound to wage war?" Liaw inquired. "Cannot the cease-fire continue until a peace treaty has been signed?"

"If that treaty gives Avalon to the Empire, will you obey?" Cajal retorted.

"Perhaps."

"Unacceptable. Best to end this affair at once." Cajal hesitated. "Of course, it will take time to set things in order everywhere else and marshal the armada here. The *de jure* cease-fire ends when my ship has returned to the agreed-on distance. But obviously the war will remain *in statu quo*, including the *de facto* cease-fire with respect to Avalon and Morgana, for a short period. I shall confer with Governor Saracoglu. I beseech you and all Avalonians to confer likewise with each other and use this respite to reach the only wise decision. Should you have any word for us, you need but broadcast a request for a parley. The sooner we hear, the milder—the more honorable—treatment you can expect."

"Observed," Liaw said. There followed ritual courtesies, and the screen blanked which had shown Cajal.

Holm and Liaw traded a look across the kilometers between them. At the rear of the man's office, Arinnian stirred uneasily.

"He means it," Holm said.

"How correct is his assessment of relative capabilities?" the Wyvan asked.

"Fairly good. We couldn't block a full-out move to wreck us. Given as many ships as he can whistle up, bombarding, ample stuff would be sure to get past our interception. We depend on the Empire's reluctance to ruin a lot of first-class real estate . . . and, yes, on that man's personal distaste for megadeaths."

"You told me earlier that you had a scheme."

"My son and I are working on it. If it shows any

promise, you and the other appropriate people will hear. Meanwhile, I imagine you're as busy as me. Fair winds, Liaw."

"Fly high, Daniel Holm." And that screen blanked.

The Marchwarden kindled a cigar and sat scowling, until he rose and went to the window. Outside was a clear winter's day. Gray did not get the snowfall of the mountains or the northern territories, and the susin stayed green on its hills the year around. But wind whooped, cold and exultant, whitecaps danced on a gunmetal bay, cloaks streamed and fluttered about walking humans, Ythrians overhead swooped through changeable torrents of air.

Arinnian joined him, but had to wet his lips before he could speak. "Dad, do we have a chance?"

"Well, we don't have a choice," Holm said.

"We do. We can swallow our damned pride and tell the people the war's lost."

"They'd replace us, Chris. You know that. Ythri could surrender because Ythri isn't being given away. The other colonies can accept occupation because it's unmistakable to everybody that they couldn't now lick a sick kitten. We're different on both counts." Holm squinted at his son through rank blue clouds of smoke. "You're not scared, are you?"

"Not for myself, I hope. For Avalon— All that rhetoric you hear about staying free. How free are corpses in a charred desert?"

"We're not preparing for destruction," Holm said. "We're preparing to risk destruction, which is something else again. The idea is to make ourselves too expensive an acquisition."

"If Avalon went to the Empire, and we didn't like the conditions, we could emigrate to the Domain."

The Marchwarden's finger traced an arc before the window. "Where would we find a mate to that? And what'd be left of this special society we, our ancestors and us, we built?"

He puffed for a minute before musing aloud: "I read a book once, on the history of colonization. The author made an interesting point. He said you've got to leave most of the surface under plant cover, rooted vegetation and phytoplankton and whatever else there may be. You need it to maintain the atmosphere. And these plants are part of an ecology, so you have to keep many animals too, and soil bacteria and so forth. Well, as long as you must have a biosphere, it's cheaper—easier, more productive—to make it supply most of your food and such, than to synthesize. That's why colonists on terrestroid worlds are nearly always farmers, ranchers, foresters, et cetera, as well as miners and manufacturers."

"So?" his son asked.

"So you grow into your world, generation by generation. It's not walls and machinery, it's a live nature, it's this tree you climbed when you were little and that field your grandfather cleared and yonder hilltop where you kissed your first girl. Your poets have sung it, your artists have drawn it, your history has happened on it, your forebears returned their bones to its earth and you will too, you will too. It is you and you are it. You can no more give it away, freely, than you could cut the heart out of your breast."

Again Holm regarded his son. "I should think you'd feel this stronger than me, Arinnian," he said. "What's got into you?"

"That man," the other mumbled. "He didn't threaten terrible things, he warned, he pleaded. That brought them home to me. I saw . . . Mother, the kids, you, my chothmates—"

*Eyath. Hrill. Hrill who is Tabitha. In these weeks we have worked together, she and Eyath and I. . . . Three days ago I flew between them, off to inspect that submarine missile base. Shining bronze wings, blowing fair hair; eyes golden, eyes green; austere jut of keelbone, heavy curve of breasts. . . . She is pure. I know she is. I make too many excuses to see her, be with her. But that damned glib Terran she keeps in her house, his tinsel cosmopolitan glamour, he hears her husky-voiced merriment oftener than I do.*

"Grant them their deathpride," Holm said.

*Eyath will die before she yields.* Arinnian straightened his shoulders. "Yes. Of course, Dad."

Holm smiled the least bit. "After all," he pointed out, "you got the first germ of this ver-r-ry intriguing notion we have to discuss."

"Actually, it . . . wasn't entirely original with me. I got talking to, uh, Tabitha Falkayn, you know her? She dropped the remark, half joking. Thinking about it later, I wondered if—well, anyhow."

"Hm. Quite a girl, seems. Especially if she can stay cheerful these days." Holm appeared to have noticed the intensity of his stare, because he turned his head quickly and said, "Let's get to work. We'll project a map first, hm?"

His thoughts could be guessed. The lift in his tone, the crinkles around his eyes betrayed them. *Well, well. Chris has finally met a woman who's not just a sex machine or a she-Ythrian to him. Dare I tell Ro, yet?— I do dare tell her that our son and I are back together.*

Around St. Li, winter meant rains. They rushed, they shouted, they washed and caressed, it was good to be out in them unclad, and when for a while they sparkled away, they left rainbows behind them.

Still, one did spend a lot of time indoors, talking or sharing music. A clear evening was not to be wasted.

Tabitha and Rochefort walked along the beach. Their fingers were linked. The air being soft, he wore simply the kilt and dagger she had given him, which matched hers.

A full Morgana lifted from eastward waters. Its

almost unblemished shield dazzled the vision with whiteness, so that what stars could be seen shone small and tender. That light ran in a quaking glade from horizon to outermost breakers, whose heads it turned into wan fire; the dunes glowed beneath it, the tops of the trees which made a shadow-wall to left became hoar. There was no wind and the surf boomed steadily and inwardly, like a heartbeat. Odors of leaf and soil overlay a breath of sea. The sands gave back the day's warmth and gritted a little as they molded themselves sensuously to the bare foot.

Rochefort said in anguish, "This to be destroyed? Burned, poisoned, ripped to flinders? And you!"

"We suppose it won't happen," Tabitha replied.

"I tell you, I *know* what's to come."

"Is the enemy certain to bombard?"

"Not willingly. But if you Avalonians, in your insane arrogance, leave no alternative—" Rochefort broke off. "Forgive me. I shouldn't have said that. It's just that the news cuts too close."

Her hand tightened on his. "I understand, Phil. You're not the enemy."

"What's bad about joining the Empire?" He waved at the sky. "Look. Sun after sun after sun. They could be yours."

She sighed. "I wish—"

She had listened in utter bewitchment to his tales of those myriad worlds.

Abruptly she smiled, a flash in the moonglow that clad her. "No, I won't wish," she said; "I'll hold you to your promise to show me Terra, Ansa, Hopewell, Cynthia, Woden, Diomedes, Vixen, every last marvel you've been regaling me with, once peace has come."

"If we're still able."

"We will be. This night's too lovely for believing anything else."

"I'm afraid I can't share your Ythrian attitude," he said slowly. "And that hurts also."

"Can't you? I mean, you're brave, I know you are, and I know you can enjoy life as it happens." Her voice and her lashes dropped. "How much you can."

He halted his stride, swung about, and caught her other hand. They stood wordlessly looking.

"I'll try," he said, "because of you. Will you help me?"

"I'll help you with anything, Phil," she answered.

They had kissed before, at first playfully as they came to feel at ease beside each other, of late more intensely. Tonight she did not stop his hands, nor her own.

"Phil and Hrill," she whispered at last, against him. "Phil and Hrill. Darling, I know a headland, a couple of kilometers further on. The trees shelter it, but you can see moon and water between them and the grass is thick and soft, the Terran grass—"

He followed her lead, hardly able to comprehend his fortune.

She laughed, a catch deep in her breast. "Yes, I planned this," she sang. "I've watched my chance for days. Mind being seduced? We may have little time in fact."

"A lifetime with you is too little," he faltered.

"Now you'll have to help me, my love, my love," she told him. "You're my first. I was always waiting for you."

# XIV

FROM the ground, Arinnian hailed Eyath. "Hoyah! Come on down and get inside." He grinned as he added in Anglic, "We Important Executives can't stall around."

She wheeled once more. Sunlight from behind turned her wings to a bronze fringed by golden haze. *She could be the sun itself,* he thought, *or the wind, or everything wild and beautiful above this ferroconcrete desert.* Then she darted at the flitter, braked in a brawl of air, and stood before him.

Her gaze fell troubled on the torpedo shape looming at his back. "Must we travel in that?" she asked.

"When we have to bounce around half a planet, yes," he replied. "You'll find it isn't bad. Especially since the hops don't take long. Less than an hour to St. Li." *To Tabby.* "Here, give me your hand."

155

She did. The fingers, whose talons could flay him, were slim and warm, resting trustfully between his. He led her up the gangway. She had flown in vehicles often before, of course, but always "eyeball" cars, frail and slow for the sake of allowing the cabins to be vitryl bubbles.

"This is a problem the choths like Stormgate, members mostly hunters, are going to have to overcome," he said. "Claustrophobia. You limit your travel capabilities too much when you insist on being surrounded by transparency."

Her head lifted. "If Vodan can suffer worse, I am ashamed I hung back, Arinnian."

"Actually, I hope you'll come to see what Vodan sees. He loves it in space, doesn't he?"

"Y-yes. He's told me that. Not to make a career of, but we do want to visit other planets after the war."

"Let's try today to convince you the journey as well as the goal is something special. . . . M-m-m, do you know, Eyath, two congenial couples traveling together— Well. Here we are."

He assisted her into harness in the copilot's seat, though she was his passenger. "Ordinarily this wouldn't be needful," he explained. "The flitter's spaceable—you could reach Morgana easily, the nearer planets if necessary—so it has counter-acceleration fields available, besides interior weight under free fall. But we'll be flying high, in the fringes of atmosphere, not to create a sonic boom. And while nothing much seems to be going on right now in the war, and we'll have a canopy of fortress orbits above us, nevertheless—"

She brushed her crest across his shoulder. "Of course, Arinnian," she murmured.

He secured himself, checked instruments, received clearance, and lifted. The initial stages were under remote control, to get him past that dance of negagrav projections which guarded the spaceport. Beyond, he climbed as fast as the law allowed, till in the upper stratosphere he fed his boat the power calculated to minimize his passage time.

"O-o-o-oh," Eyath breathed.

They were running quietly. The viewscreens gave outlooks in several directions. Below, Avalon was silver ocean. Around were purple twilight, sun, moon, a few stars: immensity, cold and serene.

"You must've seen pictures," Arinnian said.

"Yes. They're not the same." Eyath gripped his arm. "Thank you, dear galemate."

*And I'm bound for Tabby, to tell of a battle plan that may well work, that'll require we work together. How dare I be this happy?*

They flew on in the Ythrian silence which could be so much more companionable than human chatter.

There was an overcast at their destination; but when they had pierced its fog they found the sky pearl-gray, the waters white-laced indigo, the island soft green. The landing field was small, carved on the mountainside a few kilometers from the compound where Tabitha dwelt. When Chris called ahead she had promised to meet him.

He unharnessed with fingers that shook a little. Not stopping to help Eyath, he hastened to the airlock. It had opened and the gangway had extruded. A breeze ruffled his hair, warm, damp, perfumed by the janie planted around the field. Tabitha stood near, waving at him.

That was her left hand. Her right clasped the Terran's.

After half a minute she called, "Do you figure to stand there all day, Chris?"

He came down. They two released each other and extended their hands, human fashion. Meanwhile her foot caressed Rochefort's. She was wearing nothing but a few designs in body paint. They included the joyous banality of a heart pierced by an arrow.

Arinnian bowed. "We have an urgent matter to

discuss," he said in Planha. "Best we flit straight to
Draun's house."

As a matter of fact, Tabitha's partner and superior
officer was waiting in her home. "Too many young-
sters and retainers at mine," he grunted. "Secrecy
must be important, or you'd simply have phoned—
though we do see a rattlewing lot of you."

"These are always my welcome guests," the woman said
stiffly.

Arinnian wondered if the tension he felt was in the
atmosphere or his solitary mind. Draun, lean, scarred,
had not erected feathers; but he sat back on tail and
alatans in a manner suggesting surliness, and kept
stroking a dirk he wore. Tabitha's look seemed to
dwell upon Rochefort less meltingly than it had done
at the field, more in appeal.

Glancing around, Arinnian found the living room
little changed. Hitherto it had pleased him. She had
designed the house herself. The ceiling, a fluoropanel,
was low by Ythrian standards, to make the overall pro-
portions harmonious. A few susin mats lay on a floor
of polished oak, between large-windowed copperwood
walls, beneath several loungers, end tables, a stone
urn full of blossoms. While everything was clean-
scrubbed, her usual homely clutter was strewn about,
here a pipe rack and tobacco jar, there a book, yonder
a ship model she was building.

Today, however, he saw texts to inform a stranger
about Avalon, and a guitar which must have been
lately ordered since she didn't play that instrument.
The curtain had not been drawn across the doorway
to her sleeping room; Arinnian glimpsed a new wood-
and-leather-frame bed, double width.

Eyath's wing touched him. She didn't like Draun.
He felt the warmth that radiated from her.

"Yes," he said. "We do have to keep the matter
below ground." His gaze clanged on Rochefort's. "I

understand you've been studying Planha. How far along are you?"

The Terran's smile was oddly shy for an offplanet enemy who had bedazzled a girl sometimes named Hrill. "Not very," he admitted. "I'd try a few words except you'd find my accent too atrocious."

"He's doing damn well," Tabitha said, and snuggled.

His arm about her waist, Rochefort declared: "I've no chance of passing your plans on to my side, if that's what's worrying you, Citizen—uh, I mean Christopher Holm. But I'd better make my position clear. The Empire *is* my side. When I accepted my commission, I took an oath, and right now I've no way to resign that commission."

"Well said," Eyath told him. "So would my betrothed avow."

"What's honor to a Terran?" Draun snorted. Tabitha gave him a furious look. Before she could reply, Rochefort, who had evidently not followed the Planha, was proceeding:

"As you can see, I . . . expect I'll settle on Avalon after the war. Whichever way the war goes. But I do believe it can only go one way. Christopher Holm, besides falling in love with this lady, I have with her planet. Could I possibly make you consider accepting the inevitable before the horror comes down on Tabby and Avalon?"

"No," Arinnian answered.

"I thought not." Rochefort sighed. "Okay, I'll take a walk. Will an hour be long enough?"

"Oh, yes," Eyath said in Anglic.

Rochefort smiled. "I love your whole people."

Eyath nudged Arinnian. "Do you need me?" she asked. "You're going to explain the general idea. I've heard that." She made a whistling noise found solely in the Avalonian dialect of Planha—a giggle. "You know how wives flee from their husbands' jokes."

"Hm?" he said. "What'll you do?"

"Wander about with Ph . . . Phee-leep Hroash For. He has been where Vodan is."

*You too?* Arinnian thought.

"And he is the mate of Hrill, our friend," Eyath added.

"Go if you wish," Arinnian said.

"An hour, then." Claws ticked, feathers rustled as Eyath crossed the floor to the Terran. She reached up and took his arm. "Come; we have much to trade," she said in her lilting Anglic.

He smiled again, brushed his lips across Tabitha's, and escorted the Ythrian away. Silence lingered behind them, save for a soughing in the trees outside. Arinnian stood where he was. Draun fleered. Tabitha sought her pipes, chose one and began stuffing it. Her eyes held very closely on that task.

"Blame not me," Draun said. "I'd have halved him like his bald-skin fellow, if Hrill hadn't objected. Do you know she wouldn't let me make a goblet from the skull?"

Tabitha stiffened.

"Well, tell me when you tire of his bouncing you," Draun continued. "I'll open his belly on Illarian's altar."

She swung to confront him. The scar on her cheek stood bonelike over the skin. "Are you asking me to end our partnership?" tore from her. "Or to challenge you?"

"Tabitha Falkayn may regulate her own life, Draun," Arinnian said.

"Ar-r-rkh, could be I uttered what I shouldn't," the other male growled. His plumage ruffled, his teeth flashed forth. "Yet how long must we sit in this cage of Terran ships?"

"As long as need be," Tabitha snapped, still pale and shivering. "Do you want to charge out and die for naught, witless as any saga hero? Or invite the warheads that kindle firestorms across a whole continent?"

"Why not? All dies at last." Draun grinned. "What glorious pyrotechnics to go out in! Better to throw Terra onto hell-wind, alight; but since we can't do that, unfortunately—"

"I'd sooner lose the war than kill a planet, any planet," Tabitha said. "As many times sooner as it has living creatures. And I'd sooner lose this planet than see it killed." She leveled her voice and looked straight at the Ythrian. "Your trouble is, the Old Faith reinforces every wish to kill that war has roused in you—and you've no way to do it."

Draun's expression said, *Maybe. At least I don't rut with the enemy.* He kept mute, though, and Tabitha chose not to watch him. Instead she turned to Arinnian. "Can you change that situation?" she asked. Her smile was almost timid.

He did not return it. "Yes," he answered. "Let me explain what we have in mind."

Since the ornithoids did not care to walk any considerable distance, and extended conversation was impossible in flight, Eyath first led Rochefort to the stables. After repeated visits in recent weeks she knew her way about. A few zirraukhs were kept there, and a horse for Tabitha. The former were smaller than the latter and resembled it only in being warm-blooded quadrupeds—they weren't mammals, strictly speaking—but served an identical purpose. "Can you outfit your beast?" she inquired.

"Yes, now I've lived here awhile. Before, I don't remember ever even seeing a horse outside of a zoo." His chuckle was perfunctory. "Uh, shouldn't we have asked permission?"

"Why? Chothfolk are supposed to observe the customs of their guests, and in Stormgate you don't ask to borrow when you're among friends."

"How I wish we really were."

She braced a hand against a stall in order to reach

out a wing and gently stroke the pinions down his cheek.

They saddled up and rode side by side along a trail through the groves. Leaves rustled to the sea breeze, silvery-hued in that clear shadowless light. Hoofs plopped, but the damp air kept dust from rising.

"You're kind, Eyath," Rochefort said at last, awkwardly. "Most of the people have been. More, I'm afraid, than a nonhuman prisoner of war would meet on a human planet."

Eyath sought words. She was using Anglic, for the practice as much as the courtesy. But her problem here was to find concepts. The single phrase which came to her seemed a mere tautology: "One need not hate to fight."

"It helps. If you're human, anyway," he said wryly. "And that Draun—"

"Oh, he doesn't hate you. He's always thus. I feel ... pity? ... for his wife. No, not pity. That would mean I think her inferior, would it not? And she endures."

"Why does she stay with him?"

"The children, of course. And perhaps she is not unhappy. Draun must have his good points, since he keeps Hrill in partnership. Still, I will be much luckier in my marriage."

"Hrill—" Rochefort shook his head. "I fear I've earned the hate of your, uh, brother Christopher Holm."

Eyath trilled. "Clear to see, you're where he especially wanted to go. He bleeds so you can hear the splashes."

"You don't mind? Considering how close you two are."

"Well, I do not watch his pain gladly. But he will master it. Besides, I wondered if she might not bind him too closely." *Sheer off from there, lass.* Eyath regarded the man. "We gabble of what does not concern us. I would ask you about the stars you have been at, the spaces you have crossed, and what it is like to be a warrior yonder."

"I don't know," Tabitha said. "Sounds damned iffy."

"Show me the stratagem that never was," Arinnian replied. "Thing is, whether or not it succeeds, we'll have changed the terms of the fight. The Imperials will have no reason to bombard, good reason not to, and Avalon is spared." He glanced at Draun.

The fisher laughed. "Whether I wish that or not, akh?" he said. "Well, I think any scheme's a fine one which lets us kill Terrans personally."

"Are you sure they'll land where they're supposed to?" Tabitha wondered.

"No, of course we're not sure," Arinnian barked. "We'll do whatever we can to make that area their logical choice. Among other moves, we're arranging a few defections. The Terrans oughtn't to suspect they're due to us, because in fact it is not hard to get off this planet. Its defenses aren't set against objects traveling outward."

"Hm." Tabitha stroked her chin . . . big well-formed hand over square jaw, beneath heavy mouth. . . . "If *I* were a Terran intelligence officer and someone who claimed to have fled from Avalon brought me such a story, I'd put him under—what do they call that obscene gadget?—a hypnoprobe."

"No doubt." Arinnian's nod was jerky. "But these will be genuine defectors. My father has assigned shrewd men to take care of that. I don't know the details, but I can guess. We do have people who're panicked, or who want us to surrender because they're convinced we'll lose regardless. And we have more who feel that way in lesser degree, whom the first kind will trust. Suppose—well, suppose, for instance, we get President Vickery to call a potential traitor in for a secret discussion. Vickery explains that he himself wants to quit, it's political suicide for him to act openly, but he can help by arranging for certain persons to carry certain suggestions to the Terrans. Do you see? I'm not saying that's how it will be done—I really don't know how far we can trust Vickery—but we can leave the specifics to my father's men."

"And likewise the military dispositions which will make the yarn look plausible. Fine, fine," Draun gloated.

"That's what I came about," Arinnian said. "My mission's to brief the various home-guard leaders and get their efforts coordinated."

Rising from his chair, he started pacing, back and forth in front of Tabitha and never looking at her. "An extra item in your case," he went on, staccato. "It'd help tremendously if one of their own brought them the same general information."

Breath hissed between her teeth. Draun rocked forward, off his alatans, onto his toes.

"Yes," Arinnian said. "Your dear Philippe Rochefort. You tell him I'm here because I'm worried about Equatoria." He gave details. "Then I find some business in the neighbor islands and belt-flit with Eyath. Our boat stays behind, carelessly unguarded. You let him stroll freely around, don't you? His action is obvious."

Tabitha's pipestem broke in her grasp. She didn't notice the bowl fall, scattering ash and coals. "No," she said.

Arinnian found he needn't force himself to stop and glare at her as he did. "He's more to you than your world?"

"God stoop on me if ever I make use of him," she said.

"Well, if his noble spirit wouldn't dream of abusing your trust, what have you to fear?"

"I will not make my honor unworthy of his," said Hrill.

"That dungheart?" Draun gibed.

Her eyes went to him, her hand to a table beside her whereon lay a knife.

He took a backward step. "Enough," he muttered.

It was a relief when the following stillness was broken. Someone banged on the door. Arinnian, being nearest, opened it. Rochefort stood there. Behind him were a horse and a zirraukh. He breathed unevenly and blood had retreated from under his dark skin.

"You were not to come back yet," Arinnian told him.

"Eyath—" Rochefort began.

"What?" Arinnian grabbed him by the shoulders. "Where is she?"

"I don't know. I . . . we were riding, talking. . . . Suddenly she screamed. Christ, I can't get that shriek out of my head. And she took off, her wings stormed, she disappeared past the treetops before I could call to her. I . . . I waited, till—"

Tabitha joined them. She started to push Arinnian aside, noticed his stance and how his fingers dug into Rochefort's flesh, and refrained. "Phil," she said low. "Darling, think. She must've heard something terrible. What was it?"

"I can't imagine." The Terran winced under Arinnian's grip but stayed where he was. "She'd asked me to, well, describe the space war. My experiences. I was telling her of the last fight before we crash-landed. You remember. I've told you the same."

"An item I didn't ask about?"

"Well, I, I did happen to mention noticing the insigne on the Avalonian boat, and she asked how it looked."

"And?"

"I told her. Shouldn't I have?"

"What was it?"

"Three gilt stars placed along a hyperbolic curve."

Arinnian let go of Rochefort. His fist smashed into

the man's face. Rochefort lurched backward and fell to the ground. Arinnian drew his knife, started to pursue, curbed himself. Rochefort sat up, bewildered, bleeding at the mouth.

Tabitha knelt beside him. "You couldn't know, my dear," she said. Her own control was close to breaking. "What you told her was that her lover is dead."

# XV

NIGHT brought rising wind. The clouds broke apart into ragged masses, their blue-black tinged by the humpbacked Morgana which fled among them. A few stars blinked hazily in and out of sight. Surf threshed in darkness beyond the beach and trees roared in darkness ashore. The chill made humans go fully clothed.

Rochefort and Tabitha paced along the dunes. "Where *is* she?" His voice was raw.

"Alone," she answered.

"In this weather? When it's likely to worsen? Look, if Holm can go out searching, at least we—"

"They can both take care of themselves." Tabitha drew her cloak tight. "I don't think Chris really expects to find her, unless she wants to be found, and that's doubtful. He simply must do something. And he has to be away from us for a while. Her grief grieves him. It's typical Ythrian to do your first mourning by yourself."

"Saints! I've bugged things good, haven't I?"

He was a tall shadow at her side. She reached through an arm-slit, groped for and found the reality of his hand. "I tell you again, you couldn't know," she said. "Anyhow, best she learn like this, instead of dragging out more weeks or months, then never being sure he didn't die in some ghastly fashion. Now she knows he went out cleanly, too fast to feel, right after he'd won over a brave foe." She hesitated. "Besides, you didn't kill him. Our own attack did. You might say the war did, like an avalanche or a lightning stroke."

"The filthy war," he grated. "Haven't we had a gutful yet?"

Rage flared. She released him. "Your precious Empire can end it any time, you know."

"It has ended, except for Avalon. What's the sense of hanging on? You'll force them to bombard you into submission."

"Showing the rest of known space what kind of thing the Empire is. That could cost them a great deal in the long run." Tabitha's anger ebbed. *O Phil, my only!* "You know we're banking on their not being monsters, and on their having a measure of enlightened self-interest. Let's not talk about it more."

"I've got to. Tabby, you and Holm—but it's old Holm, of course, and a few other old men and Ythrians, who don't care how many young die as long as they're spared confessing their own stupid, senile willfulness—"

"Stop. Please."

"I can't. You're mounting some crazy new plan you think'll let your one little colony hold off all those stars. I say to the extent it works, it'll be a disaster.

Because it may prolong the fight, sharpen it— No, I can't stand idly by and let you do that to yourself."

She halted. He did likewise. They peered at each other through the unrestful wan light. "Don't worry," she said. "We know what we're about."

"Do you? What is your plan?"

"I mustn't tell you that, darling."

"No," he said bitterly, "but you can let me lie awake nights, you can poison my days, with fear for you. Listen, I know a fair amount about war. And about the psychology of the Imperial high command. I could give you a pretty good guess at how they'd react to whatever you tried."

Tabitha shook her head. She hoped he didn't see her teeth catching her lip.

"Tell me," he insisted. "What harm can I do? And my advice— Or maybe you don't propose anything too reckless. If I could be sure of that—"

She could barely pronounce it: "Please. Please."

He laid hands on her shoulders. Moonlight fell into his eyes, making them blank pools. "If you love me, you will," he said.

She stood in the middle of the wind. *I can't lie to him. Can I? But I can't break my oath either. Can I?*

*What Arinnian wanted me to tell him—*

*But I'm not testing you, Phil, Phil. I'm . . . choosing the lesser evil . . . because you wouldn't want your woman to break her oath, would you? I'm giving you what short-lived happiness I can, by an untruth that won't make any difference to your behavior. Afterward, when you learn, I'll kneel to ask your forgiveness.*

She was appalled to hear from her throat: "Do we have your parole?"

"Not to use the information against you?" His voice checked for a fractional second. Waves hissed at his back. "Yes."

"Oh, no!" She reached for him. "I never meant—"

"Well, you have my word, sweetheart mine."

*In that case—* she thought. *But no, I couldn't tell him the truth before I'd consulted Arinnian, who'd be sure to say no, and anyhow Phil would be miserable, in terror for me and, yes, for his friends in their navy, whom honor would not let him try to warn.*

She clenched her fists, beneath the flapping cloak, and said hurriedly: "Well, in fact it's nothing fundamental. You know about Equatoria, the uninhabited continent. Nothing's there except a few thinly scattered emplacements and a skeleton guard. They mostly sit in barracks, because that few trying to patrol that much territory is pointless. Chris has been worried."

"Hm, yes, I've overheard him mention it to you."

"He's gotten his father to agree the defenses are inadequate. In particular, making a close study, they found the Scorpeluna tableland's wide open. Surrounding mountains, air turbulence, and so forth isolate it. An enemy who concentrated on breaking through the orbital fortresses and coming down fast— as soon as he was below fifty kilometers, he'd be shielded from what few rays we can project, and he could doubtless handle what few missiles and aircraft we could send in time. Once on the ground, dug in— you savvy? Bridgehead. We want to strengthen the area. That's all."

She stopped. Dizziness grabbed her. *Did I talk on a single breath?*

"I see," he responded after a while. "Thank you, dearest."

She came to him and kissed him, tenderly because of his hurt mouth.

Later that night the wind dropped, the clouds regathered, and rain fell, slow as tears. By dawn it was used up. Laura rose blindingly out of great waters, into utter blue, and every leaf and blade on the island was jeweled.

Eyath left the crag whereon she had perched the last few hours, after she could breast the weather no more. She was cold, wet, stiff at first. But the air blew keen into nostrils and antlibranchs, blood awoke, soon muscles were athrob.

*Rising, rising,* she thought, and lifted herself in huge upward spirals. The sea laughed but the island dreamed, and her only sound was the rush which quivered her pinions.

*At your death, Vodan, you too were a sun.*

Despair was gone, burned out by the straining of her wings, buffeted out by winds and washed out by rain, as he would have demanded of her. She knew the pain would be less quickly healed; but it was nothing she could not master. Already beneath it she felt the sorrow, like a hearthfire at which to warm her hands. Let a trace remain while she lived; let Vodan dwell on in her after she had come to care for another and give that later love his high-heartedness.

She tilted about. From this height she saw more than one island, strewn across the mercury curve of the world. *I don't want to return yet, Arinnian can await me till ... dusk?* Hunger boiled in her. She had consumed a great deal of tissue. *Bless the pangs, bless this need to hunt—bless the chance, ha!*

Far below, specks, a flock of pteropleuron left their reef and scattered in search of piscoids near the water surface. Eyath chose her prey, aimed and launched herself. When she drew the membranes across her eyes to ward them, the world blurred and dimmed somewhat; but she grew the more aware of a cloven sky streaming and whistling around her; claws which gripped the bend of either wing came alive to every shift of angle, speed, and power.

Her body knew when to fold those wings and fall— when to open them again, brake in thunder, whip on

upward—when and how her hands must strike. Her
dagger was not needed. The reptiloid's neck snapped
at the sheer violence of that meeting.

*Vodan, you'd have joyed!*

Her burden was handicapping; not heavy, it had
nonetheless required wide foils to upbear it. She settled on an offshore rock, butchered the meat and ate.
Raw, it had a mild, almost humble flavor. Surf shouted
and spouted around her.

Afterward she flew inland, slowly now. She would
seek the upper plantations and rest among trees and
flowers, in sun-speckled shade; later she would go
back aloft; and all the time she would remember
Vodan. Since they had not been wedded, she could
not lead his funeral dance; so today she would give
him her own, their own.

She skimmed low above an orchard. Water, steaming off leaves and ground, made small white mists
across the green, beneath the sun. Upwelling currents
stroked her. She drank the strong odors of living earth
through antlibranchs as well as lungs, until they made
her lightheaded and started a singing in her blood.
*Vodan,* she dreamed, *were you here beside me, we
would flit off, none save us. We would find a place for
you to hood me in your wings.*

It was as if he were. The beating that closed in from
behind and above, the air suddenly full of maleness.
Her mind spun. *Am I about to faint? I'd better set
down.* She sloped unevenly and landed hard.

Orange trees stood around, not tall nor closely
spaced, but golden lanterns glowed mysteriously in the
deeps of their leafage. The soil was newly weeded and
cultivated, bare to the sky. Its brown softness
embraced her feet, damp, warmed by the sun that
dazzled her. Light torrented down, musk and sweet-
ness up, and roared.

Pinions blotted out Laura for a moment. The other
descended. She knew Draun.

His crest stood stiff. Every quill around the grinning mouth said: *I hoped I might find you like this, after what's happened.*

"No," she whimpered, and spread her wings to fly.

Draun advanced stiffly over the ground, arms held wide and crook-fingered. "Beautiful, beautiful," he hawked. "Khr-r-r."

Her wings slapped. The inrush of air brought strength, but not her own strength. It was a different force that shook her as she might shake a prey.

"Vodan!" she yelled, and somehow flapped off the whirling earth. The lift was slow and clumsy. Draun reached up, hooked foot-claws around an alatan of hers; they tumbled together.

She scratched at his face and groped for her knife. He captured both wrists and hauled her against him. "You don't really want that, you she," his breath gusted in her ear. "Do you now?" He brought her arms around his neck and he himself hugged her. Spread, his wings again shut out the sun, before their plumes came over her eyes.

Her clasp held him close, her wings wrapped below his. She pressed her lids together so hard that dark was full of dancing formless lights. *Vodan,* passed somewhere amidst the noise, *I'll pretend he's you.*

But Vodan would not have gone away afterward, leaving her clawed, bitten, and battered for Arinnian to find.

Tabby was still asleep, Holm still looking for his poor friend, Draun lately departed with a remark about seeing if he couldn't help, the retainers and fishers off on their various businesses. The compound lay quiet under the morning.

Rochefort stole back into the bedroom. She was among the few women he'd known who looked good at this hour. The tall body, the brown skin were too firm to sag or puff; the short fair locks tangled in a way that begged his fingers to play games. She breathed deeply, steadily, no snoring though the lips were a little parted over the whiteness beneath. When he bent above her, through bars of light and shade cast by the blind, she had no smell of sourness, just of girl. He saw a trace of dried tears.

His mouth twisted. The broken lip twinged less than his heart. She'd cried on *his* account, after they came home. "Of course you can't tonight, darling," she'd whispered, leaning over him on an elbow and running the other hand down cheek and breast and flank. "With this trouble, and you pulled ninety different ways, and everything. You'd be damned callous if you could, how 'bout that? Don't you cry. You don't know how, you make it too rough on yourself. Wait till tomorrow or the next night, Phil, beloved. We've got a lifetime."

*A large subdivision of my hell was that I couldn't tell you why I was taking it so hard,* he thought.

*If I kiss you . . . but you might wake and— O all you saints, St. Joan who burned for her people, help me!*

The knowledge came that if he dithered too long, she would indeed wake. He gave himself a slow count of one hundred before he slipped back out.

The roofs of the buildings, the peak beyond them, stood in impossible clarity against a sky which a pair of distant wings shared with the sun. The softest greens and umbers shone no less than the most brilliant red. The air was drenched in fragrances of growth and of the sea which tumbled beyond the breakwater. *No. This much beauty is unendurable.* Rochefort walked fast from the area, onto a trail among the orchards. Soon it would join the main road to the landing field.

*I can't succeed. Someone'll be on guard; or I'll be unable to get in; or something'll happen and I'll simply have been out for a stroll. No harm in looking, is there?*

*Merely looking and returning for breakfast. No harm in that, except for letting her Avalonians be killed, maybe by millions, maybe including her—and, yes, my shipmates dying too—uselessly, for no reason whatsoever except pride—when maybe they can be saved. When maybe she'll see that I did what I did to end the war quickly that she might live.*

The country lay hushed. Nobody had work on the plantations this time of year.

The landing field was deserted. For as scanty traffic as St. Li got, automated ground control sufficed.

The space flitter stood closed. Rochefort strangled on relief till he remembered: *Could be against no more than weather. They have no worries about thieves here.*

*How about curious children?*

*If somebody comes along and sees me, I can explain I got worried about that. Tabby will believe me.*

He wheeled a portable ramp, used for unloading cargo carriers, to the sleek hull. Mounting, his boots went knock . . . knock . . . knock. The entrance was similar to kinds he had known and he found immediately a plate which must cover an exterior manual control. It was not secured, it slid easily aside, and behind was nothing keyed to any individual or signal, only a button. He pressed it. The outer valve purred open and a gangway came forth like a licking tongue.

*Father, show me Your will.* Rochefort stepped across and inside.

The Ythrian vessel was quite similar to her Terran counterparts. No surprise, when you considered that the flying race learned spaceflight from man, and that on Avalon their craft must often carry humans. In the pilot room, seats and controls were adjustable for either species. The legends were in Planha, but

Rochefort puzzled them out. After five minutes he knew he could lift and navigate this boat.

He smote palm into fist, once. Then he buckled down to work.

# XVI

ARINNIAN carried Eyath back to the compound on foot. His gravbelt wouldn't safely raise them both and he left it behind. Twice she told him she could fly, or walk at any rate, but in such a weak whisper that he said, "No." Otherwise they did not speak, after the few words she had coughed against his breast while he knelt to hold her.

He couldn't carry that mass long in his arms. Instead, she clung to him, keelbone alongside his back, foot-claws curved over his shoulders, hugging his waist, like a small Ythrian child except that he must help her against the heaviness of the planet by his clasp on her alatans. He had cut his shirt into rags to sponge her hurts with rainwater off the leaves, and into bandages to stop further bleeding. The injuries weren't clinically serious, but it gave him something to use his knife on. Thus the warmth (the heat) and silk featheriness of her lay upon his skin; and the smell of her lovetime, like heavy perfume, was around him and in him.

*That's the worst,* he kept thinking. *The condition'll last for days—a couple of weeks, given reinforcement. If she encounters him again—*

*Is she remorseful? How can she be, for a thing she couldn't halt? She's stunned, of course, harmed, dazed; but does she feel mortally befouled? Ought she to?*

*Suddenly I don't understand my galemate.*

He trudged on. There had been scant rest for him during his search. He ached, his mouth was dry, his brain seemed full of sand. The world was a path he had to walk, so-and-so many kilometers long, except that the kilometers kept stretching. This naturally thinned the path still more, until the world had no room left for anything but a row of betrayals. He tried to shut out consciousness of them by reciting a childish chant in his head for the benefit of his feet. "You *pick* 'em *up* an' *lay* 'em *down*. You *pick* 'em *up*—" But this made him too aware of feet, how they hurt, knees, how they shivered, arms, how they burned, and perforce he went back to the betrayals. Terra-Ythri. Ythri-Avalon. Tabitha-Rochefort. Eyath-Draun, no, Draun-Eyath . . . Vodan-whatsername, that horrible creature in Centauri, yes, Quenna . . . Eyath-anybody, because right now she was anybody's . . . no, a person had self-control, forethought, a person could stay chaste if not preserve that wind-virginity which had been hers. . . . Those hands clasped on his belly, which had lain in his, had lately strained to pull Draun closer; that voice which had sung to him, and was now stilled, had moaned like the voice of any slut—*Stop that! Stop, I say!*

Sight of the compound jarred him back to a sort of reality. No one seemed about. Luck. He'd get Eyath

safely put away. Ythrian chemists had developed an
aerosol which effectively nullified the pheromones,
and doubtless some could be borrowed from a neighbor. It'd keep the local males from strutting and gawk-
ing outside her room, till she'd rested enough to fly
with him to the boat and thence home to Stormgate.

Tabitha's house stood open. She must have heard
his footsteps and breath, for she came to the door.
"Hullo," she called. "You found her? . . . Hoy!" She
ran. He supposed once he would have appreciated the
sight. "She okay?"

"No." He plodded inside. The coolness and shade
belonged to a different planet.

Tabitha padded after. "This way," she suggested.
"My bed."

"No!" Arinnian stopped. He would have shrugged
if he weren't burdened. "Why not?"

Eyath lay down, one wing folded under her, the
other spread wide so the pinions trailed onto the floor.
The nictitating membranes made her appear blind.
"Thank you." She could barely be heard.

"What happened?" Tabitha bent to see. The odor
that a male Ythrian could catch across kilometers
reached her. "Oh." She straightened. Her jaw set.
"Yeh."

Arinnian sought the bathroom, drank glass after
glass of cold water, showered beneath the iciest of the
needle-spray settings. That and a stimpill brought him
back to alertness. Meanwhile Tabitha went in and out,
fetching supplies for Eyath's care.

When they were both finished, they met in the living room. She put her lips close to his ear—he felt
the tiny puffs of her words—to say very low: "I gave
her a sedative. She'll be asleep in a few minutes."

"Good," he answered out of his hatred. "Where's
Draun?"

Tabitha stepped back. The green gaze widened.
"Why?"

"Can't you guess? Where is he?"

"Why do you want Draun?"

"To kill him."

"You won't!" she cried. "Chris, if it was him, they couldn't help themselves. Neither could. You know that. Shock and grief brought on premature ovulation, and then he chanced by—"

"He didn't chance by, that slime," Arinnian said. "Or if he did, he could've veered off from the first faint whiff he got, like any decent male. He most certainly didn't have to brutalize her. Where is he?"

Tabitha moved sidewise, in front of the phone. She had gone paler than when Draun mocked her. He shoved her out of his way. She resisted a moment, but while she was strong, she couldn't match him. "At home, you've guessed," Arinnian said. "A bunch of friends to hand, armed."

"To keep you from trying anything reckless, surely, surely," Tabitha pleaded. "Chris, we've a war. He's too important in the guard. We— If Phil were here you'd never— Must I go after a gun?"

He sat down. "Your stud couldn't prevent me calling from a different place," he snapped. She recoiled. "Nor could your silly gun. Be quiet."

He knew the number and stabbed it out. The screen came to life: Draun and, yes, a couple more in the background, blasters at their sides. The Ythrian spoke at once: "I expected this. Will you hear me? Done's done, and no harm in it. Choth law says not, in cases like this, save that a gild may be asked for wounded pride and any child must be provided for. There'll hardly be a brat, from this early in her season, and as for pride, she enjoyed herself." He grinned and stared past the man. "Didn't you, prettytail?"

Arinnian craned his neck around. Eyath staggered from the bedroom. Her eyes were fully open but glazed by the drug which had her already half unconscious. Her arms reached toward the image in the screen. "Yes. Come," she croaked. "No. Help me, Arinnian. Help."

He couldn't move. It was Tabitha who went to her and led her back out of sight.

"You see?" Draun said. "No harm. Why, you humans can force your females, and often do, I've heard. I'm not built for that. Anyhow, what's one bit of other folk's sport to you, alongside your hundred or more each year?"

Arinnian had kept down his vomit. It left a burning in his gullet. His words fell dull and, in his ears, remote, though every remaining sense had become preternaturally sharp. "I saw her condition."

"Well, maybe I did get a bit excited. Your fault, really, you humans. We Ythrians watch your ways and begin to wonder. You grip my meaning? All right, I'll offer gild for any injuries, as certified by a medic. I'll even discuss a possible pride-payment, with her parents, that is. Are you satisfied?"

"No."

Draun bristled his crest a little. "You'd better be. By law and custom, you've no further rights in the matter."

"I'm going to kill you," Arinnian said.

"What? Wait a wingbeat! Murder—"

"Duel. We've witnesses here. I challenge you."

"You've no cause, I say!"

Arinnian could shrug, this time. "Then you challenge me."

"What for?"

The man sighed. "Need we plod through the formalities? Let me see, what deadly insults would fit? The vulgarism about what I can do when flying above you? No, too much a cliché. I'm practically compelled to present a simple factual description of your character, Draun. Thereto I will add that Highsky Choth is a clot of dung, since it contains such a maggot."

"Enough," the Ythrian said, just as quietly though

his feathers stood up and his wings shuddered. "You are challenged. Before my gods, your gods, the memory of all our forebears and the hope of all our descent, I, Draun of Highsky, put you, Christopher Holm, called Arinnian of Stormgate, upon your death-pride to meet me in combat from which no more than one shall go alive. In the presence and honor of these witnesses whom I name—"

Tabitha came from behind. By force and surprise, she hauled Arinnian off his chair. He fell to the floor, bounced erect, and found her between him and the screen. Her left hand fended him off, her right was held as if likewise to keep away his enemy, her partner.

"Are you both insane?" she nearly screamed.

"The words have been uttered." Draun peeled his fangs. "Unless he beg grace of me."

"I would not accept a plea for grace from him," Arinnian said.

She stood panting, swinging her head from each to each. The tears poured down her face; she didn't appear to notice. After some seconds her arms dropped, her neck drooped.

"Will you hear me, then?" she asked hoarsely. They held still. Arinnian had begun to tremble under a skin turning cold. Tabitha's fists closed where they hung. "It's not to your honor that you let th-th-those persons your choths ... Avalon ... needs ... be killed or, or crippled. Wait till war's end. I challenge you to do that."

"Well, aye, if I needn't meet nor talk to the Walker," Draun agreed reluctantly.

"If you mean we must cooperate as before," Arinnian said to Tabitha, "you'll have to be our go-between."

"How can she?" Draun jeered. "After the way you bespoke her choth."

"I think I can, somehow," Hrill sighed.

She stood back. The formula was completed. The screen blanked.

Strength poured from Arinnian. He turned to the girl and said, contrite, "I didn't mean that last. Of you I beg grace, to you I offer gild."

She didn't look his way, but sought the door and stared outward. *Toward her lover,* he thought vaguely. *I'll find a tree to rest beneath till Eyath rouses and I can transport her to the flitter.*

A crash rolled down the mountainside and rattled the windows. Tabitha grew rigid. The noise toned away, more and more faint as the thunderbolt fled upward. She ran into the court. "Phil!" she shouted. *Ah,* Arinnian thought. *Indeed. The next betrayal.*

"At ease, Lieutenant. Sit down."

The dark, good-looking young man stayed tense in the chair. Juan Cajal dropped gaze back to desk and rattled the papers in his hands. Silence brimmed his office cabin. *Valenderay* swung in orbit around Pax at a distance which made that sun no more than the brightest of the stars, whose glare curtained Esperance where Luisa waited.

"I have read this report on you, including the transcription of your statements, with care, Lieutenant Rochefort," Cajal said finally, "long though it be. That's why I had you sent here by speedster."

"What can I add, sir?" The newcomer's voice was stiff as his body. However, when Cajal raised his look to meet those eyes again, he remembered a gentle beast he had once seen on Nuevo México, in the Sierra de los Bosques Secos, caught at the end of a canyon and waiting for the hunters.

"First," the admiral said, "I want to tender my personal apology for the hypnoprobing to which you were subjected when you rejoined our fleet. It was no way to treat a loyal officer."

"I understand, sir," Rochefort said. "I wasn't surprised,

and the interrogators were courteous. You had to be sure I wasn't lying." Briefly, something flickered behind the mask. "To you."

"M-m, yes, the hypnoprobe evokes every last detail, doesn't it? The story will go no further, son. You saw a higher duty and followed."

"Why fetch me in person, sir? What little I had to tell must be in that report."

Cajal leaned back. He constructed a friendly smile. "You'll find out. First I need a bit of extra information. What do you drink?"

Rochefort started. "Sir?"

"Scotch, bourbon, rye, gin, tequila, vodka, akvavit, et cetera, including miscellaneous extraterrestrial bottles. What mixes and chasers? I believe we've a reasonably well-stocked cabinet aboard." When Rochefort sat dumb, Cajal finished: "I like a martini before dinner myself. We're dining together, you realize."

"I am? The, the admiral is most kind. Yes. A martini. Thanks."

Cajal called in the order. Actually he took a small sherry, on the rare occasions when he chose anything; and he suspected Rochefort likewise had a different preference. But it was important to get the boy relaxed.

"Smoke?" he invited. "I don't, but I don't mind either, and the governor gave me those cigars. He's a noted gourmet."

"Uh . . . thank you . . . not till after eating, sir."

"Evidently you're another." Cajal guided the chit-chat till the cocktails arrived. They were large and cold. He lifted his. "*A vuestra salud, mi amigo.*"

"Your health—" The embryo of a smile lived half a second in Rochefort's countenance. "*Bonne santé, Monsieur l'Amiral.*"

They sipped. "Go ahead, enjoy," Cajal urged. "A man of your proven courage isn't afraid of his supreme boss. Your immediate captain, yes, conceivably; but not me. Besides, I'm issuing you no orders. Rather, I asked for what help and advice you care to give."

Rochefort had gotten over being surprised. "I can't imagine what, sir." Cajal set him an example by taking a fresh sip. Cajal's, in a glass that bore his crest, had been watered.

Not that he wanted Rochefort drunk. He did want him loosened and hopeful.

"I suppose you know you're the single prisoner to escape," the admiral said. "Understandable. They probably hold no more than a dozen or two, from boats disabled like yours, and you were fabulously lucky. Still, you may not know that we've been getting other people from Avalon."

"Defectors, sir? I heard about discontent."

Cajal nodded. "And fear, and greed, and also more praiseworthy motives, a desire to make the best of a hopeless situation and avoid further havoc. They've been slipping off to us, one by one, a few score total. Naturally, all were quizzed, even more thoroughly than you. Your psychoprofile was on record; Intelligence need merely establish it hadn't been tampered with."

"They wouldn't do that, sir," Rochefort said. Color returned to his speech. "About the worst immorality you can commit on Avalon is stripping someone else of his basic honor. That costs you yours." He sank back and took a quick swallow. "Sorry, sir."

"Don't apologize. You spoke in precisely the vein I wish. Let me go on, though. The first fugitives hadn't much of interest to tell. Of late— Well, no need for lectures. One typical case will serve. A city merchant, grown rich on trade with nearby Imperial worlds. *He* won't mind us taking over his planet, as long as the war doesn't ruin his property and the aftermath cost him extra taxes. Despicable, or realistic? No matter. The point is, he possessed certain information, and had certain other information given him to pass on, by quite highly placed officials who're secretly of the peace group."

Rochefort watched Cajal over the rim of his glass. "You fear a trap, sir?"

Cajal spread his palms. "The fugitives' sincerity is beyond doubt. But were they fed false data before they left? Your story is an important confirmation of theirs."

"About the Equatorian continent?" Rochefort said. "No use insulting the admiral's intelligence. I probably would not have tried to get away if I didn't believe what I'd heard might be critical. However, I know very little."

Cajal tugged his beard. "You know more than you think, son. For instance, our analysis of enemy fire patterns, as recorded at the first battle of Avalon does indicate Equatoria is a weak spot. Now you were on the scene for months. You heard them talk. You watched their faces, faces of people you'd come to know. How concerned would you say they really were?"

"Um-m-m. . . ." Rochefort drank anew. Cajal unobtrusively pressed a button which signaled the demand for a refill for him. "Well, sir, the, the lady I was with, Equatoria was out of her department." He hastened onward: "Christopher Holm, oldest son of their top commander, yes, I'd say he worried about it a lot."

"What's the place like? Especially this, ah, Scorpeluna region. We're collecting what information we can, but with so many worlds around, who that doesn't live on them cares about their desert areas?"

Rochefort recommended a couple of books. Cajal didn't remind him that Intelligence's computers must have retrieved these from the libraries days or weeks ago. "Nothing too specific," the lieutenant went on. "I've gathered it's a large, arid plateau, surrounded by mountains they call high on Avalon, near the middle of the continent, which the admiral knows isn't big.

Some wild game, perhaps, but no real hope of living off the country." He stopped for emphasis. "Counter-attackers couldn't either."

"And they, who have oceans to cross, would actually be further from home than our people from our ships," Cajal murmured.

"A dangerous way down, sir."

"Not after we'd knocked out the local emplace-ments. And those lovely, sheltering mountains—"

"I thought along the same lines, sir. From what I know of, uh, available production and transportation facilities, and the generally sloppy Ythrian organiza-tion, they can't put strong reinforcements there fast. Whether or not my escape alarms them."

Cajal leaned over his desk. "Suppose we did it," he said. "Suppose we established a base for aircraft and ground-to-ground missiles. What do you think the Avalonians would do?"

"They'd have to surrender, sir," Rochefort answered promptly, "They . . . I don't pretend to understand the Ythrians, but the human majority—well, my impres-sion is that they'll steer closer to a *Götterdämmerung* than we would, but they aren't crazy. If we're there, on land, if we can shoot at everything they have, not in an indiscriminate ruin of their beloved planet—that prospect is what keeps them at fighting pitch—but if we can do it selectively, laying our own bodies on the line—" He shook his head. "My apologies. That got tangled. Besides, I could be wrong."

"Your impressions bear out every xenological study I've seen," Cajal told him. "Furthermore, yours come from a unique experience." The new drink arrived. Rochefort demurred. Cajal said: "Please do take it. I want your free-wheeling memories, your total aware-ness of that society and environment. This is no easy decision. What you can tell me certainly won't make up my mind by itself. However, any fragment of fact I can get, I must."

Rochefort regarded him closely. "You want to invade, don't you, sir?" he asked.

"Of course. I'm not a murder machine. Neither are my superiors."

"I want us to. Body of Christ"— Rochefort signed himself before the crucifix—"how I want it!" He let his glass stand while he added: "One request, sir. I'll pass on everything I can. But if you do elect this operation, may I be in the first assault group? You'll need some Meteors."

"That's the most dangerous, Lieutenant," Cajal warned. "We won't be sure they have no hidden reserves. Therefore we can't commit much at the start. You've earned better."

Rochefort took the glass, and had it been literally that instead of vitryl, his clasp would have broken it. "I request precisely what I've earned, sir."

# XVII

THE Imperial armada englobed Avalon and the onslaught commenced.

Once more ships and missiles hurtled, energy arrows flew, fireballs raged and died, across multiple thousands of kilometers. This time watchers on the ground saw those sparks brighten, hour by hour, until at last they hurt the eyes, turned the world momentarily livid and cast stark shadows. The fight was moving inward.

* * *

Nonetheless it went at a measured pace. Cajal had hastened his decision and brought in his power as fast as militarily possible—within days—lest the enemy get time to strengthen that vulnerable country of theirs. But now that he was here, he took no needless risks.

189

Few were called for. This situation was altogether different from the last. He had well-nigh thrice his former might at hand, and no worries about what relics of the Avalonian navy might still skulk through the dark reaches of the Lauran System. Patrols reported instrumental indications that these were gathering at distances of one or two astronomical units. Since they showed no obvious intention of casting themselves into the furnace, he saw no reason to send weapons after them.

He did not even order the final demolition of Ferune's flagship, when the robots within knew their foe and opened fire. She was floating too distantly, she had too little ammunition or range left her, to be worth the trouble. It was easier to bypass the poor old hulk and the bones which manned her.

Instead he concentrated on methodically reducing the planetary defense. Its outer shell was the fortresses, some great, most small, on sentry-go in hundreds of orbits canted at as many angles to the ecliptic. They had their advantages *vis-à-vis* spaceships. They could be continually resupplied from below. Nearly all of them wholly automated, they were less versatile but likewise less fragile than flesh and nerve. A number of the least had gone undetected until their chance came to lash out at a passing Terran.

That, though, had been at the first battle. Subsequently the besieging sub-fleet had charted each, destroyed no few and forestalled attempts at replacement. Nor could the launching of salvos from the ground be again a surprise. And ships in space had their own advantages, e.g., mobility.

Cajal's general technique was to send squadrons by at high velocity and acceleration. As they entered range of a target they unleashed what they had and immediately applied unpredictable vectors to escape return fire. If the first pass failed, a second quickly followed, a third, a fourth . . . until defense was saturated and the station exploded in vapor and shards. Having no cause now to protect his rear or his supply lines, Cajal could be lavish with munitions, and was.

Spacecraft in that kind of motion were virtually hopeless goals for missiles which must rise through atmosphere, against surface gravity, from zero initial speed. The Avalonians soon realized as much and desisted for the time being.

Cajal's plan did not require the preliminary destruction of every orbital unit. That would have been so expensive that he would have had to hang back and wait for more stocks from the Empire; and he was in a hurry. He did decide it was necessary to neutralize the moon, and for a while Morgana was surrounded and struck by such furies that mountains crumbled and valleys ran molten.

Otherwise, on the whole, the Imperials went after those fortresses which, in their ever-changing configurations, would menace his first landing force on the date set by his tactical scheme. In thus limiting his objective, he was enabled to focus his full energies sharply. Those incandescent hours, running into a pair of Avalonian days, were the swiftest penetration ever made of defenses that strong.

Inevitably, he took losses. The rate grew when his ships started passing so close above the atmosphere that ground-based projectors and missile sites became effective. The next step was to nullify certain of these, together with certain other installations.

\* \* \*

Captain Ion Munteanu, commanding fire control aboard H.M.S. *Phobos,* briefed his officers while the ship rushed forward.

"Ours is a special mission, as you must have guessed from this class of vessel being sent. We aren't just going to plaster a spot that's been annoying the boys. We're after a city. I see a hand. Question, Ensign Ozumi?"

"Yes, sir. Two. How and why? We can loose enough torps and decoys, sophisticated enough, that if we keep it up long enough, a few are bound to duck in and around the negafields and burst where they'll do some good. That's against a military target. But surely they've given their cities better protection than that."

"I remind you about eggs and grandmothers, Ensign. Of course they have. Powerful, complicated set-ups, plus rings of exterior surface-to-space launchers. We'll be firing our biggest and best, programmed for detonation at high substratospheric altitude. The pattern I'm about to diagram should allow one, at least, to reach that level before it's intercepted. If not, we start over."

"Sir! You don't mean a continent buster!"

"No, no. Calm down. Remember this ship couldn't accommodate any. We have no orders to damage His Majesty's real estate beyond repair. Ours will be heavy brutes, true, but clean, and shaped to discharge their output straight ahead, mainly in the form of radiation. Blast wouldn't help much against the negafields. We'll whiff the central part of town, and Intelligence tells me the fringes are quite flammable."

"Sir, I don't want to annoy you, but why do we do it?"

"Not wantonly, Ozumi. A landing is to be made. Planetside warfare may go on for a while. This particular town, Centauri they call it, is their chief seaport and industrial capital. We are not going to leave it to send stuff against our friends."

Sweat stood on Ozumi's brow. "Women and children—"

"If the enemy has any sense, he evacuated nonessential persons long ago," Munteanu snapped. "Frankly, I don't give a curse. I lost a brother here, last time around. If you're through sniveling, let's get to work."

Quenna flapped slowly above the Livewell Street canal. Night had fallen, a clear night unlike most in the Delta's muggy winters. Because of that and the blackout, she could see stars. They frightened her. Too many of the cold, nasty little things. And they weren't only that, she was told. They were suns. War came from them, war that screwed up the world.

Fine at first, lots of Ythrians passing through, jingle in their purses, moments when she forgot all except the beauty of the male and her love for him; in between, she could afford booze and dope to keep her happy, especially at parties. Parties were a human idea, she'd heard. (Who was it had told her? She tried to remember the face, the body. She would be able to, if they didn't blur off into the voices and music and happy-making smoke.) A good idea. Like war had seemed. Love, love, love, laugh, laugh, laugh, sleep, sleep, sleep, and if you wake with your tongue tasting bad and needles in your head, a few pills will soon put you right.

Except it went sour. No more navy folk. The Nest empty, a cave, night after night after night, till a lass was ready to scream except that the taped music did that for her. Most humans moving out, too, and those who stayed—she'd even have welcomed human company—keeping underground. The black, quiet nights, the buzzing aloneness by day, the money bleeding off till she could barely buy food, let alone a bottle or a pill to hold off the bad dreams.

Flap, flap, Somebody must be in town and lonesome, now the fighting had started again. "I'm lonesome too," she called. "Whoever you are, I love you." Her voice sounded too loud in this unmoving warm air, above these oily waters and dead pavements, between those shadowy walls and beneath those terrible little stars.

"Vodan?" she called more softly. She remembered him best of the navy folk, almost as well as the first few who had used her, more years back than she cared to count. He'd been gentle and bothered about his lass at home, as if that dragglewing deserved him. But she was being silly, Quenna was. No doubt the stars had eaten Vodan.

She raised her crest. She had her deathpride. She would not be frightened in the midnight streets. Soon dawn would break and she could dare sleep.

The sun came very fast.

She had an instant when it filled the sky. Night caught her then, as her eyeballs melted. She did not know this, because her plumage was on fire. Her scream drowned out the following boom, when superfast molecules of air slipped by the negafields, and she did not notice how it ruptured eardrums and smashed capillaries. In her delirium of pain, there was nothing except the canal. She threw herself toward it, missed, and fell into a house which stood in one blaze. That made no difference, since the canal waters were boiling.

Apart from factors of morale and war potential, the strike at Centauri must commit a large amount of Avalonian resources to rescue and relief. It had been well timed. A mere three hours later, the slot which had been prepared in the defenses completed itself and the first wave of invasion passed through.

Rochefort was in the van. He and his hastily assembled crew had had small chance to practice, but they were capable men and the Meteor carried out her assignment with an *élan* he wished he could feel. They ran interference for the lumbering gunships till these were below the dangerous altitude. En route, they stopped a pair of enemy missiles. Though no spacecraft was really good in atmosphere, a torpedo boat combined acceptable maneuverability, ample firepower, and more than ample wits aboard. Machines guided by simple robots were no match.

Having seen his charges close to ground, Rochefort took his vessel, as per assignment, against the source of the missiles. It lay beyond the mountains, in the intensely green gorge of a river. The Terran boats roared one after the next, launched beams and torpedoes against negafields and bunkers, stood on their tails and sprang to the stratosphere, swept about and returned for the second pass. No third was needed. A set of craters gaped between cliffs which sonic booms had brought down in rubble. Rochefort wished he could forget how fair that canyon had been.

Returning to Scorpeluna, he found the whole convoy landed. Marines and engineers were swarming from personnel transports, machines from the freighters. Overhead, patrol craft darkened heaven. They were a frantic few days that followed. Hysteria was never far below the skin of purposeful activity. Who knew for certain what the enemy had?

Nothing came. The screen generators were assembled and started. Defensive projectors and missiles were positioned. Sheds were put together for equipment, afterward for men. And no counterattack was made.

Airborne scouts and spaceborne instruments reported considerable enemy activity on the other continents and across the islands. Doubtless something was being readied. But it didn't appear to pose any immediate threat.

The second slot opened. The second wave flowed down, entirely unopposed. Scorpeluna Base spread like an inkblot.

His intention now being obvious, Cajal had various other orbital fortresses destroyed, in order that slots come more frequently. Thereafter he pulled his main fleet back a ways. From it he poured men and equipment groundward.

The last Avalonian ships edged nearer, fled from sorties, returned to slink about, wolves too starveling to be a menace. No serious effort was wasted on them. The essential was to exploit this tacit cease-fire while it lasted. On that account, the Imperials everywhere refrained from offensive action. They worked at digging in where they were and at building up their conquest until it could not merely defend itself, it could lift an irresistible fist above all Avalon.

Because he was known to have the favor of the grand admiral, Lieutenant Philippe Rochefort (newly senior grade) got his application for continued planetside duty approved. Since there was no further call for a space torpedo craft, he found himself flying aerial patrol in a two-man skimmer, a glorified gravsled.

His assigned partner was a marine corporal, Ahmed Nasution, nineteen standard years old, fresh off New Djawa and into the corps. "You know, sir, everybody told me this planet was a delight," he said, exaggerating his ruefulness to make sure his superior got the point. "Join the navy and see the universe, eh?"

"This area isn't typical," Rochefort answered shortly.

"What is," he added, "on an entire world?"

The skimmer flew low above the Scorpelunan plateau. The canopy was shut against broiling air. A Hilsch tube arrangement and self-darkening vitryl did their inadequate best to combat that heat, brazen sky, bloated and glaring sun. The only noises were hum of engine, whirr of passage. Around the horizon stood mountain peaks, dim blue and unreal. Between reached emptiness. Bushes, the same low, reddish-leaved, medicinal-smelling species wherever you looked, grew widely apart on hard red earth. The land was not really flat. It raised itself in gnarly mesas and buttes, it opened in great dry gashes. At a distance could be seen a few six-legged beasts, grazing in the shade of their parasol membranes. Otherwise nothing stirred save heat shimmers and dust devils.

"Any idea when we'll push out of here?" Nasution asked, reaching for a water bottle.

"When we're ready," Rochefort told him. "Easy on the drink. We've several hours to go, you and I."

"Why doesn't the enemy give in, sir? A bunch of us in my tent caught a 'cast of theirs—no orders not to, are there?—a 'cast in Anglic. I couldn't understand it too well, their funny accent and, uh, phrases like 'the Imperials have no more than a footgrip,' you have to stop and figure them out and meanwhile the talking goes on. But Gehenna, sir, we don't *want* to hurt them. Can't they be reasonable and—"

"Sh!" Rochefort lifted an arm. His monitoring radio identified a call. He switched to that band.

*"Help! O God, help!*— Engineer Group Three . . . wild animals . . . estimate thirty-four kilometers north-northwest of camp— *Help!"*

Rochefort slewed the skimmer about.

He arrived in minutes. The detail, ten men in a groundcar, had been running geological survey to determine the feasibility of blasting and fuse-lining a large missile silo. They were armed, but had looked for no troubles except discomfort. The pack of dog-sized hexapodal lopers found them several hundred meters from their vehicle.

Two men were down and being devoured. Three had scattered in terror, seeking to reach the car, and been individually surrounded. Rochefort and Nasution saw one overwhelmed. The rest stood firm, back to back, and maintained steady fire. Yet those scaly-bristly shapes seemed almost impossible to kill. Mutilated, they dragged their jaws onward.

Rochefort yelled into his transmitter for assistance, swooped, and cut loose. Nasution wept but did good work at his gun. Nevertheless, two more humans were lost before the lycosauroids had been slain.

After that, every group leaving camp got an aerial escort, which slowed operations elsewhere.

"No, Doctor, I've stopped believing it's psychogenic." The major glanced out of the dispensary shack window, to an unnaturally swift sunset which a dust storm made the color of clotted blood. Night would bring relief from the horrible heat ... in the form of inward-gnawing chill. "I was ready to believe that at first. Your psychodrugs aren't helping any longer, though. And more and more men are developing the symptoms, as you must know better than I. Bellyache, diarrhea, muscle pains, more thirst than this damned dryness will account for. Above all, tremors and fuzzy-headedness. I hate to tell you how necessary a job I botched today."

"I'm having my own troubles thinking." The medical officer passed a hand across his temple. It left a streak of grime, despite the furnace air sucking away sweat before that could form drops. "Frequent blurred vision too? Yes."

"Have you considered a poison in the environment?"

"Certainly. You weren't in the first wave, Major. I was. Intelligence, as well as history, assured us Avalon is acceptably safe. Still, take my word, we'd scarcely established camp when the scientific team was checking."

"How about quizzing Avalonian prisoners?"

"I'm assured this was done. In fact, there've been subsequent commando operations just to collect more for that purpose. But how likely are any except a few specialists to know details about the most forbidding part of a whole continent that nobody inhabits?"

"And of course the Avalonians would have all those experts safely tucked out of reach." The major gusted a weary breath. "So what did your team find?"

The medical officer groped for a stimpill out of the open box on his desk. "There is a, ah, high concentration of heavy metals in local soil. But nothing to worry about. You could breathe the dust for years before you'd require treatment. The shrubs around use those elements in their metabolism, as you'd expect, and we've warned against chewing or burning any part of them. No organic compounds test out as allergens.

Look, human and Ythrian biochemistries are so similar the races can eat most of each other's food. If this area held something spectacularly deadly, don't you imagine the average colonist would have heard of it, at least? I'm from Terra—middle west coast of North America—oh, Lord—" For a while his gaze was gone from Scorpeluna. He shook himself. "We lived among oleanders. We cultivated them for their flowers. Oleanders are poisonous. You just need to be sensible about them."

"This has got to have some cause," the major insisted.

"We're investigating," the medic said. "If anyone had foreseen this planet would amount to anything militarily—it'd have been studied before ever we let a war happen, so thoroughly— Too late."

Occasional small boats from the Avalonian remnants slipped among the Terran blockaders at high ve'...ity and maximum variable acceleration. About half were destroyed; the rest got through and returned spaceward. It was known that they exchanged messages with the ground. Given suitable encoding and laser beams, a huge amount of information can be passed in a second or two.

"Obviously they're discussing a move," Cajal snarled at his staff. "Equally obviously, if we try to hunt them, they'll scatter and vanish in sheer distance, sheer numbers of asteroids and moons, same's they did before. And they'll have contingency plans. I do not propose to be diverted, gentlemen. We shall keep our full strength here."

For a growing body of observations indicated that, on land and sea, under sea and in their skies, the colonists were at last making ready to strike back.

Rochefort heard the shrieking for the better part of a minute before it registered on him. *Dear Jesus,* dragged through his dullness, *what ails me?* His muscles protested bringing the skimmer around. His fingers were sausages on the control board. Beside him, Nasution slumped mute, as the boy had been these past days (weeks? years?). The soft cheeks had collapsed and were untidily covered by black down.

Still, Rochefort's craft arrived to help those which had been floating above a ground patrol. The trouble was, it could then do no more than they. Energy weapons incinerated at a flash hundreds of the cockroach-like things, twenty centimeters long, whose throngs blackened the ground between shrubs. They could not save the men whom these bugs had already reached and were feasting on. Rochefort carefully refrained from noting which skimmer pilots gave, from above, a *coup de grace*. He himself hovered low and hauled survivors aboard. After what he had seen, in his present physical shape, Nasution was too sick to be of use.

Having evidently gotten wind of meat in this hungry land, the kakkelaks swarmed toward the main base. They couldn't fly, but they clattered along astonishingly fast. Every effort must go to flaming a cordon against them.

Meanwhile the Avalonians landed throughout Equatoria. They deployed so quickly and widely—being very lightly equipped—that bombardment would have been futile. All who entered Scorpeluna were Ythrian.

The chief officers of medicine and planetology confronted their commandant. Outside, an equinoctial gale bellowed and rang through starless night; dust scoured over shuddering metal walls. The heat seemed to come in enormous dry blasts.

"Yes, sir," the medical chief said. Being regular navy rather than marine, he held rear admiral's rank. "We've proven it beyond reasonable doubt." He sighed, a sound lost in the noise. "If we'd had better equipment, more staff— Well, I'll save that for the board of inquiry, or the court-martial. The fact is, poor information got us sucked into a death trap."

"Too many worlds." The civilian planetologist shook his gaunt head. "Each too big. Who can know?"

"While you gabble," the commandant said, "men lie in delirium and convulsions. More every day. Talk." His voice was rough with anger and incomplete weeping.

"We suspected heavy-metal poisoning, of course," the medical officer said. "We made repeated tests. The concentration always seemed within allowable limits. Then over night—"

"Never mind that," the planetologist interrupted. "Here are the results. These bushes growing everywhere around . . . we knew they take up elements like arsenic and mercury. And the literature has described the hell shrub, with pictures, as giving off dangerous vapors. What we did not know is that here *is* a species of hell shrub. It looks entirely unlike its relatives. Think of roses and apples. Besides, we'd no idea how the toxin of the reported kind works, let alone these. That must have been determined after the original descriptions were published, when a purely organic compound was assumed. The volume of information in every science, swamping—" His words limped to a halt.

The commandant waited.

The medical officer took the tale: "The vapors carry the metals in loose combination with a . . . a set of molecules, unheard of by any authority I've read. Their action is, well, they block certain enzymes. In effect, the body's protections are canceled. No metal atoms whatsoever are excreted. Every microgram goes to the vital organs. Meanwhile the patient is additionally weakened by the fact that parts of his protein chemistry aren't working right. The effects are synergistic and exponential. Suddenly one crosses a threshold."

"I . . . see . . ." the commandant said.

"We top officers aren't in too bad a condition yet," the planetologist told him. "Nor are our staffs. We spend most of our time indoors. The men, though—" He rubbed his eyes. "Not that I'd call myself a well man," he mumbled.

"What do you recommend?" the commandant asked.

"Evacuation," the medical chief said. "And I don't recommend it, I tell you we have no alternative. Our people must get immediate proper care."

The commandant nodded. Himself sick, monstrously tired, he had expected some such answer days ago and started his quiet preparations.

"We can't lift off tomorrow," he said in his dragging tones. "We haven't the bottom; most's gone back to space. Besides, a panicky flight would make us a shooting gallery for the Avalonians. But we'll organize to raise the worst cases, while we recall everybody to the main camp. We'll have more ships brought down, in orderly fashion." He could not control the twitch in his upper lip.

As the Imperials retreated, their enemies struck.

They fired no ground-to-ground missiles. Rather, their human contingents went about the construction of bases which had this capability, at chosen spots throughout the Equatorian continent. It was not difficult. They were only interested in short-range weapons, which needed little more than launch racks, and in aircraft, which needed little more than maintenance shacks for themselves and their crews. The largest undertaking was the assembly of massive energy projectors in the peaks overlooking Scorpeluna.

Meanwhile the Ythrians waged guerrilla warfare on the plateau. They, far less vulnerable to the toxicant peculiar to it, were in full health and unburdened by the spacesuits, respirators, handkerchiefs which men frantically donned. Already winged, they need not sit in machines which radar, gravar, magnetoscopes could spot across kilometers. Instead they could dart from what cover the ground afforded, spray a trudging column with fire and metal, toss grenades at a vehicle, sleet bullets through any skimmers, and be gone before effective reaction was possible.

Inevitably, they had their losses.

"Hya-a-a-ah!" yelled Draun of Highsky, and swooped from a crag down across the sun-blaze. At the bottom of a dry ravine, a Terran column stumbled toward camp from a half-finished emplacement. Dust turned every man more anonymous than what was left of his uniform. A few armored groundcars trundled among them, a few aircraft above. A gravsled bore rapidly mummifying corpses, stacked.

"Cast them onto hell-wind!" The slugthrower stuttered in Draun's grasp. Recoil kept trying to hurl him off balance, amidst these wild thermals. He gloried that his wings were too strong and deft for that.

The Ythrians swept low, shooting, and onward. Draun saw men fall like emptied sacks. Wheeling beyond range, he saw their comrades form a square, anchored by its cars and artillery, helmeted by its flyers. *They're still brave,* he thought, and wondered if they hadn't best be left alone. But the idea had been to push them into close formation, then on the second pass drop a tordenite bomb among them. "Follow me!"

The rush, the bullets and energy bolts, the appallingly known wail at his back. Draun braked, came about, saw Nyesslan, his oldest son, the hope of his house, spiral to ground on a wing and a half. The Ythrian squadron rushed by. *"I'm coming, lad!"* Draun glided down beside him. Nyesslan lay unconscious. His blood purpled the dust. The second attack failed, broke up in confusion before it won near to the square. True to doctrine, that they should hoard their numbers, the Ythrians beat back out of sight.

A platoon trotted toward Draun. He stood above Nyesslan and fired as long as he was able.

"Take out everything they have remaining in orbit," Cajal said. "We need freedom to move our transports continuously."

His chief of staff cleared throat. "Hr-r-rm, the admiral knows about the hostile ships?"

"Yes. They're accelerating inward. It's fairly clear that all which can make planetfall hope to do so; the rest are running interference."

"Shouldn't we organize an interception?"

"We can't spare the strength. Clearing away those forts will empty most of our magazines. Our prime duty is to pull our men out of that mess we ... I ... sent them into." Cajal stiffened himself. "If any units can reasonably be spared from the orbital work, yes, let them collect what Avalonians they can, provided they conserve munitions to the utmost and rely mainly on energy weapons. I doubt they'll get many. The rest we'll have to let go their ways, perhaps to our sorrow." His chuckle clanked. "As old Professor Wu-Tai was forever saying at the Academy—remember, Jim?—'The best foundation that a decision is ever allowed is our fallible assessment of the probabilities.'"

The tropical storms of Avalon were more furious than one who came from a planet of less irradiation and slower spin could well have imagined. For a day and a night, the embarkation of the sickest men was postponed. Besides the chance of losing a carrier, there was a certainty that those flensing rains would kill some of the patients as they were borne from shacks to gangways.

The more or less hale, recently landed, battled to erect levees. Reports, dim and crackling through radio static, were of flash floods leaping down every arroyo.

Neither of these situations concerned Rochefort. He

was in an intermediate class, too ill for work, too well for immediate removal. He huddled on a chair among a hundred of his fellows, in a stinking, steaming bunker, tried to control the chills and nausea that went ebb-and-flow through him, and sometimes thought blurrily of Tabitha Falkayn and sometimes of Ahmed Nasution, who had died three days before.

What Avalonian spacecraft ran the gantlet descended to Equatoria, where home-guard officers assigned them their places.

The storm raged to its end. The first Imperial vessels lifted from the wrecked base. They were warships, probing a way for the crammed, improvised hospital hulls which were to follow. Sister fighters moved in from orbit to join them.

Avalon's ground and air defenses opened crossfire. Her space force entered battle.

Daniel Holm sat before a scanner. It gave his words and his skull visage to the planet's most powerful linked transmitters, a broadcast which could not fail to be heard:

"—we're interdicting their escape route. You can't blast us in time to save what we estimate as a quarter million men. Even if we didn't resist, maybe half of them would never last till you brought them to adequate care. And I hate to think about the rest—organ, nerve, brain damage beyond the power of regenerative techniques to heal.

"*We* can save them. We of Avalon. We have the facilities prepared, clear around our planet. Beds, nursing staffs, diagnostic equipment, chelating drugs, supportive treatments. We'd welcome your inspection teams and medical personnel. Our wish is not to play political games with living people. The minute you agree to renew the ceasefire and to draw your fleet far enough back that we can count on early warning, that same minute our rescue groups will take flight for Scorpeluna."

# XVIII

THE ward was clean and well-run, but forty men must be crowded into it and there was no screen—not that local programs would have interested most of them. Hence they had no entertainment except reading and bitching. A majority preferred the latter. Before long, Rochefort asked for earcups in order that he might be able to use the books lent him. He wore them pretty much around the clock.

Thus he did not hear the lickerish chorus. His first knowledge came from a touch on his shoulder. *Huh?* he thought. *Lunch already?* He raised his eyes from *The Gaiila Folk* and saw Tabitha.

The heart sprang in him and raced. His hands shook so he could barely remove the cups.

She stood athwart the noisy, antiseptic-smelling room as if her only frame were a window behind, open to the blue and blossoms of springtime. A plain coverall disguised the curves and straightness of her. He saw in the countenance that she had lost weight. Bones stood forth still more strongly than erstwhile, under a skin more darkened and hair more whitened by a stronger sun than shone over Gray.

"Tabby," he whispered, and reached.

She took his hands, not pressing them nor smiling much. "Hullo, Phil," said the remembered throaty voice. "You're looking better'n I expected, when they told me you'd three tubes in you."

"You should have seen me at the beginning." He heard his words waver. "How've you been? How's everybody?"

"I'm all right. Most of those you knew are. Draun and Nyesslan bought it."

"I'm sorry," he lied.

Tabitha released him. "I'd have come sooner," she said, "but had to wait for furlough, and then it took time to get a data scan on those long lists of patients and time to get transportation here. We've a lot of shortages and disorganization yet." Her regard was green and grave. "I did feel sure you'd be on Avalon, dead or alive. Good to learn it was alive."

"How could I stay away . . . from you?"

She dropped her lids. "What is your health situation? The staff's too busy to give details."

"Well, when I'm stronger they want to ship me to a regular Imperial navy hospital, take out my liver and grow me a new one. I may need a year, Terran, to recover completely. They promise me I will."

"Splendid." Her tone was dutiful. "You being well treated here?"

"As well as possible, considering. But, uh, my roommates aren't exactly my type and the medics and helpers, both Imperial and Avalonian, can't stop their work for conversation. It's been damned lonesome, Tabby, till you came."

"I'll try to visit you again. You realize I'm on active duty, and most of what leave I'm granted has to be spent at St. Li, keeping the business in shape."

Weakness washed through him. He leaned back into the pillows and let his arms fall on the blanket. "Tabby . . . would you consider waiting . . . that year?"

She shook her head, slowly, and again met his stare. "Maybe I ought to pretend till you're more healed, Phil. But I'm no good at pretending, and besides, you rate better."

"After what I did—"

"And what I did." She leaned down and felt past the tubes to lay palms on his shoulders. "No, we've never hated on that account, have we, either of us?"

"Then can't we both forgive?"

"I believe we've already done it. Don't you see, though? When the hurting had died down to where I could think, I saw there wasn't anything left. Oh, friendship, respect, memories to cherish. And that's all."

"It isn't enough . . . to rebuild on?"

"No, Phil. I understand myself better than I did before. If we tried, I know what sooner or later I'd be doing to you. And I won't. What we had, I want to keep clean."

She kissed him gently and raised herself.

They talked awhile longer, embarrassed, until he could dismiss her on the plea, not entirely untruthful, that he needed rest. When she was gone he did close his eyes, after donning the earcups which shut out the Terran voices.

*She's right, probably,* he thought. *And my life isn't blighted. I'll get over this one too, I suppose.* He recalled a girl in Fleurville and hoped he would be

transferred to an Esperancian hospital, when or if the
cease-fire became a peace.

Outside, Tabitha stopped to put on the gravbelt she
had retrieved from the checkroom. The building had
been hastily erected on the outskirts of Gray. (She
remembered the protests when Marchwarden Holm
diverted industrial capacity from war production to
medical facilities, at a time when renewed combat
seemed imminent. Commentators pointed out that
what he had ordered was too little for the casualties
of extensive bombardment, too much for those of any
plausible lesser-scale affray. He had growled, "We do
what we can" and rammed the project through. It
helped that the principal home-guard officers urged
obedience to him. They knew what he really had in
mind—these men whose pain kept the weapons
uneasily silent.) Where she stood, a hillside sloped
downward, decked with smaragdine susin, starred with
chasuble bush and Buddha's cup, to the strewn and
begardened city, the huge curve of uprising shoreline,
the glitter on Falkayn Bay. Small cottony clouds saun-
tered before the wind, which murmured and smelled of
livewell.

She inhaled that coolness. After Equatoria, it was
intoxicating. Or it ought to be. She felt curiously
empty.

Wings boomed. An Ythrian landed before her.
"Good flight to you, Hrill," the female greeted.

Tabitha blinked. Who—? Recognition came. "Eyath!
To you, good landing." *How dull her tone, how
sheenless her plumes. I haven't seen her since that day
on the island. . . .* Tabitha caught a taloned hand in
both of hers. "This is wonderful, dear. Have you been
well?"

Eyath's stance and feathers and membranes drawn
over her eyes gave answer. Tabitha hunkered down
and embraced her.

"I sought you," Eyath mumbled. "I spent the battle at home; afterward too, herding, because I needed aloneness and they told me the planet needs meat." Her head lay in Tabitha's bosom. "Lately I've been freed of that and came to seek—"

Tabitha stroked her back, over and over.

"I learned where you were posted and that you'd mentioned you would stop in Gray on your furlough," Eyath went on. "I waited. I asked of the hotels. Today one said you had arrived and gone out soon after. I thought you might have come here, and trying was better than more waiting."

"What little I can do for you, galemate, tell me."

"It is hard." Eyath clutched Tabitha's arms, painfully, without raising her head. "Arinnian is here too. He has been for some while, working on his father's staff. I sought him and—" A strangled sound, though Ythrians do not weep.

Tabitha foresaw: "He avoids you."

"Yes. He tries to be kind. That is the worst, that he must try."

"After what happened—"

"Ka-a-a-ah. I am no more the same to him." Eyath gathered her will. "Nor to myself. But I hoped Arinnian would understand better than I do."

"Is he the solitary one who can help? What of your parents, siblings, chothmates?"

"They have not changed toward me. Why should they? In Stormgate a, a misfortune like mine is reckoned as that, a misfortune, no disgrace, no impairment. They cannot grasp what I feel."

"And you feel it because of Arinnian. I see." Tabitha looked across the outrageously lovely day. "What can I do?"

"I don't know. Maybe nothing. Yet if you could speak to him—explain—beg grace of him for me—"

Anger lifted. "*Beg* him? Where is he?"

"At work, I, I suppose. His home—"

"I know the address." Tabitha released her and stood up. "Come, lass. No more talk. We're off for a good hard flight in this magnificent weather, and I'll take advantage of being machine-powered to wear you out, and at day's end we'll go to wherever you're staying and I'll see you asleep."

—Twilight fell, saffron hues over silver waters, elsewhere deep blue and the earliest stars. Tabitha landed before Arinnian's door. His windows glowed. She didn't touch the chime plate, she slammed a panel with her fist.

He opened. She saw he had also grown thin, mahogany hair tangled above tired features and disheveled clothes. "Hrill!" he exclaimed. "Why . . . I never—Come in, come in."

She brushed past him and whirled about. The chamber was in disarray, obviously used only for sleeping and bolted meals. He moved uncertainly toward her. Their contacts had been brief, correct, and by phone until the fighting began. Afterward they verified each other's survival, and that was that.

"I'm, I'm glad to see you, Hrill," he stammered.

"I don't know as I feel the same," she rapped. "Sit down. I've got things to rub your nose in, you sanctimonious mudbrain."

He stood a moment, then obeyed. She saw the strickenness upon him and abruptly had no words. They looked, silent, for minutes.

Daniel Holm sat before the screens which held Liaw of The Tarns, Matthew Vickery of the Parliament, and Juan Cajal of the Empire. A fourth had just darkened. It had carried a taped plea from Trauvay, High Wyvan of Ythri, that Avalon yield before worse should befall and a harsher peace be dictated to the whole Domain.

"You have heard, sirs?" Cajal asked.

"We have heard," Liaw answered.

Holm felt the pulse in his breast and temples, not much quickened but a hard, steady slugging. He longed for a cigar—unavailable—or a drink—unadvisable—or a year of sleep—unbroken. *At that,* crossed his mind, *we're in better shape than the admiral. If ever I saw a death's head, it rides his shoulderboards.*

"What say you?" Cajal went on like an old man.

"We have no wish for combat," Liaw declared, "or to deepen the suffering of our brethren. Yet we cannot give away what our folk so dearly bought for us."

"Marchwarden Holm?"

"You won't renew the attack while we've got your people here," the human said roughly. "Not that we'll hold them forever. I told you before, we don't make bargaining counters out of thinking beings. Still, the time and circumstances of their release have to be negotiated."

Cajal's glance shifted to the next screen. "President Vickery?"

A politician's smile accompanied the response: "Events have compelled me to change my opinion as regards the strategic picture, Admiral. I remain firm in my opposition to absolutist attitudes. My esteemed colleague, Governor Saracoglu, has always impressed me as being similarly reasonable. You have lately returned from a prolonged conference with him. Doubtless many intelligent, well-informed persons took part. Did no possibility of compromise emerge?"

Cajal sagged. "I could argue and dicker for days," he said. "What's the use? I'll exercise my discretionary powers and lay before you at once the maximum I'm authorized to offer."

Holm gripped the arms of his chair.

"The governor pointed out that Avalon can be considered as having already met most terms of the armistice," crawled from Cajal. "Its orbital fortifications no longer exist. Its fleet is a fragment whose sequestration, as required, would make no real difference to you. Most important, Imperial units *are* now on your planet.

"Nothing is left save a few technicalities. Our wounded and our medics must be given the acknowledged name of occupation forces. A command must be established over your military facilities; one or two men per station will satisfy that requirement while posing no threat of takeover should the truce come apart. Et cetera. You see the general idea."

"The saving of face," Holm grunted. "Uh-huh. Why not? But how about afterward?"

"The peace treaty remains to be formulated," said the drained voice. "I can tell you in strict confidence, Governor Saracoglu has sent to the Imperium his strongest recommendation that Avalon not be annexed."

Vickery started babbling. Liaw held stiff. Holm gusted a breath and sat back.

They'd done it. They really had.

The talk would go on, of course. And on and on and on, along with infinite petty particulars and endless niggling. No matter. Avalon would stay Ythrian—stay free.

*I ought to whoop,* he thought. *Maybe later. Too tired now.*

His immediate happiness, quiet and deep, was at knowing that tonight he could go home to Rowena.

# XIX

THERE were no instant insights, no dramatic revelations and reconciliations. But Arinnian was to remember a certain hour.

His work for his father had stopped being very demanding. He realized he should use the free time he had regained to phase back into his studies. Then he decided that nothing was more impractical than misplaced practicality. Tabitha agreed. She got herself put on inactive duty. Eventually, however, she must return to her island and set her affairs in order, if only for the sake of her partner's family. Meanwhile he was still confined to Gray.

He phoned Eyath at her rented room: "Uh, would you, uh, care to go for a sail?"

*Yes*, she said with every quill.

Conditions were less than perfect. As the boat left the bay, rain came walking. The hull skipped over choppy olive-dark waves, tackle athrum; water slanted from hidden heaven, long spears which broke on the skin and ran down in cool splinters, rushing where they entered the sea.

"Shall we keep on?" he asked.

"I would like to." Her gaze sought land, a shadow aft. No other vessels were abroad, nor any flyers. "It's restful to be this alone."

He nodded. He had stripped, and the cleanness dwelt in his hair and sluiced over his flesh.

She regarded him from her perch on the cabin top, across the cockpit which separated them. "You had something to tell me," she said with two words and her body.

"Yes." The tiller thrilled between his fingers. "Last night, before she left—" In Planha he need speak no further.

"Galemate, galemate," she breathed. "I rejoice." She half extended her wings toward him, winced, and withdrew them.

"For always," he said in awe.

"I could have wished none better than Hrill, for you," Eyath replied. Scanning him closer: "You remain in fret."

He bit his lip.

Eyath waited.

"Tell me," he forced forth, staring at the deck. "You see us from outside. Am I able to be what she deserves?"

She did not answer at once. Startled not to receive the immediate yea he had expected, Arinnian lifted his eyes to her silence. He dared not interrupt her thought. Waves boomed, rain laughed.

Finally she said, "I believe she is able to make you able."

He nursed the wound. Eyath began to apologize, summoned resolution and did not. "I have long felt," she told him, "that you needed someone like Hrill to show you that—show you how—what is wrong for my folk is right, is the end and meaning of life, for yours."

He mustered his own courage to say, "I knew the second part of that in theory. Now she comes as the glorious fact. Oh, I was jealous before. I still am, maybe I will be till I die, unable to help myself. She, though, she's worth anything it costs. What I am learning, Eyath, my sister, is that she is not you and you are not her, and it is good that you both are what you are."

"She has given you wisdom." The Ythrian hunched up against the rain.

Arinnian saw her grief and exclaimed, "Let me pass the gift on. What befell you—"

She raised her head to look wildly upon him.

"Was that worse than what befell her?" he challenged. "I don't ask for pity"—human word—"because of past foolishness, but I do think my lot was more hard than either of yours, the years I wasted imagining bodily love can ever be bad, imagining it has any real difference from the kind of love I bear to you, Eyath. Now we'll have to right each other. I want you to share my hopes."

She sprang down from the cabin, stumbled to him and folded him in her wings. Her head she laid murmuring against his shoulder. Raindrops glistened within the crest like jewels of a crown.

The treaty was signed at Fleurville on a day of late winter. Little ceremony was involved and the Ythrian delegates left almost at once. "Not in very deep anger," Ekrem Saracoglu explained to Luisa Cajal, who had declined his invitation to attend. "By and large, they take their loss philosophically. But we couldn't well ask them to sit through our rituals." He drew on his cigaret. "Frankly, I too was glad to get off that particular hook."

He had, in fact, simply made a televised statement and avoided the solemnities afterward. A society like Esperance's was bound to mark the formal end of hostilities by slow marches and slower thanksgiving services.

That was yesterday. The weather continued mild on this following afternoon, and Luisa agreed to come to dinner. She said her father felt unwell, which, regardless of his liking and respect for the man, did not totally displease Saracoglu.

They walked in the garden, she and he, as often before. Around paths which had been cleared, snow decked the beds, the bushes and boughs, the top of the wall, still white although it was melting, here and there making thin chimes and gurgles as the water ran. No flowers were left outdoors, the air held only dampness, and the sky was an even dove-gray. Stillness lay beneath it, so that footfalls scrunched loud on gravel.

"Besides," he added, "it was a relief to see the spokesman for Avalon and his cohorts board their ship. The secret-service men I'd assigned to guard them were downright ecstatic."

"Really?" She glanced up, which gave him a chance to dwell on luminous eyes, tip-tilted nose, lips always parted as if in a child's eagerness. But she spoke earnestly—too earnestly, too much of the time, damn it. "I knew there had been some idiot anonymous death threats against them. Were you that worried?"

He nodded. "I've come to know my dear Esperancians. When Avalon dashed their original jubilation— well, you've seen and heard the stuff about 'intransigent militarists.'" He wondered if his fur cap hid his baldness or reminded her of it. Maybe he should break down and get a scalp job.

Troubled, she asked, "Will they ever forget . . . both sides?"

"No," he said. "I do expect grudges will fade. We've too many mutual interests, Terra and Ythri, to make a family fight into a blood feud. I hope."

"We *were* more generous than we had to be. Weren't we? Like letting them keep Avalon. Won't that count?"

"It should." Saracoglu grinned on the left side of his mouth, took a final acrid puff and tossed his cigaret away. "Though everybody sees the practical politics involved. Avalon proved itself indigestible. Annexation would have spelled endless trouble, whereas Avalon as a mere enclave poses no obvious difficulties such as the war was fought to terminate. Furthermore, by this concession, the Empire won some valuable points with respect to trade that might otherwise not have been feasible to insist on."

"I know," she said, a bit impatiently.

He chuckled. "You also know I like to hear myself talk."

She grew wistful. "I'd love to visit Avalon."

"Me too. Especially for the sociological interest. I wonder if that planet doesn't foreshadow the distant future."

"How?"

He kept his slow pace and did not forget her arm resting on his; but he squinted before him and said out of his most serious thought, "The biracial culture they're creating. Or that's creating itself; you can't plan or direct a new current in history. I wonder if that wasn't the source of their resistance—like an alloy or a two-phase material, many times stronger than either part that went into it. We've a galaxy, a cosmos to fill—"

*My, what a mixed bag of metaphors, including this one,* gibed his mind. He laughed inwardly, shrugged outwardly, and finished: "Well, I don't expect to be around for that. I don't even suppose I'll have to meet the knottier consequences of leaving Avalon with Ythri."

"What could those be?" Luisa wondered. "You just said it was the only thing to do."

"Indeed. I may be expressing no more than the natural pessimism of a man whose lunch at Government House was less than satisfactory. Still, one can imagine. The Avalonians, both races, are going to feel themselves more Ythrian than the Ythrians. I anticipate future generations of theirs will supply the Domain with an abnormal share, possibly most of its admirals. Let us hope they do not in addition supply it with revanchism. And under pacific conditions, Avalon, a unique world uniquely situated, is sure to draw more than its share of trade—more important, brains, which follow opportunity. The effects of that are beyond foreseeing."

Her clasp tightened on his sleeve. "You make me glad I'm not a statesman."

"Not half as glad as I am that you're not a statesman," he said, emphasizing the last syllable. "Come, let's drop these dismal important matters. Let's discuss—for example, your tour of Avalon. I'm sure it can be arranged, a few months hence."

She turned her face from him. When the muteness had lasted a minute, he stopped, as did she. "What's the matter?" he asked, frightened.

"I'm leaving, Ekrem," she said. "Soon. Permanently."

"What?" He restrained himself from seizing her.

"Father. He sent in his resignation today."

"I know he . . . has been plagued by malicious accusations. You recall I wrote to Admiralty Center."

"Yes. That was nice of you." She met his eyes again.

"No more than my duty, Luisa." The fear would not leave him, but he was pleased to note that he spoke firmly and maintained his second-best smile. "The Empire needs good men. No one could have predicted the Scorpeluna disaster, nor done more after the thing happened than Juan Cajal did. Blaming him, calling for court-martial, is wizened spite, and I assure you nothing will come of it."

"But he blames himself," she cried low.

*I have no answer to that,* he thought.

"We're going back to Nuevo México," she said.

"I realize," he attempted, "these scenes may be unduly painful to him. Need you leave, however?"

"Who else has he?"

"Me. I, ah, will presumably get an eventual summons to Terra—"

"I'm sorry, Ekrem." Her lashes dropped over the delicate cheekbones. "Terra would be no good either. I won't let him gnaw away his heart alone. At home, among his own kind, it will be better." She smiled, not quite steadily, and tossed her head. "*Our* kind. I admit a little homesickness myself. Come visit us sometime." She chose her words: "No doubt I'll be getting married. I think, if you don't mind, I think I'd like to name a boy for you."

"Why, I would be honored beyond anything the Emperor could hang on this downward-slipping chest of mine," he said automatically. "Shall we go inside? The hour's a trifle early for drinks, perhaps; on the other hand, this is a special occasion."

*Ah, well,* he thought above the pain, *the daydream was a pleasant guest, but now I am freed from the obligations of a host. I can relax and enjoy the games of governor, knight, elevated noble, Lord Advisor, retired statesman dictating interminable and mendacious memoirs.*

*Tomorrow I must investigate the local possibilities*

*with respect to bouncy and obliging ladies. After all, we are only middle-aged once.*

Summer dwelt in Gray when word reached Avalon. There had been some tension—who could really trust the Empire?—and thus joy amid the human population exploded in festival.

Bird, Christopher Holm and Tabitha Falkayn soon left the merriment. Announcements, ceremonies, feasts could wait; they had decided that the night of final peace would be their wedding night.

Nonetheless they felt no need of haste. That was not the way of the choths. Rather, two sought to become one with their world, their destiny, and their dead—whether in waiting for lovetime or in love itself—until all trouble had been mastered and they could freely become one with each other.

Beyond the northern headland, the hills were as yet uninhabited, though plants whose ancestral seeds arrived with the pioneers had here long ceased to be foreign. Chris and Tabby landed in a sunset whose red and gold ran berserk above a quiet sea. They pitched camp, ate, drank a small glass of wine and a long kiss; afterward, hand in hand, they walked a trail which followed the ridge.

On their left, as daylight smoldered away, grasses wherein clustered trefoil and sword-of-sorrow fell steeply down to the waters. These glimmered immense, out to a horizon which lost itself in a sky deepening from violet to crystalline black. The evening star stood as a candle among the awakening constellations. On their right was forest, darkling, still sweet from odors of pine. A warm small breeze made harp vines ring and brightness twinkle among the jewelleafs.

"Eyath?" she asked once.

"Homebound," he answered.

That, and his tone and the passage of his mouth

across her dimly seen hair, said: *In showing me I must heal her, and how, you healed me, my darling.*

Her fingertips, touching his cheek, said: *To my own gladness, which grew and grew.*

Nevertheless he sensed a question in her. He thought he knew what it was. It had often risen in him; but he, the reader, philosopher, poet, could inquire of the centuries better than she, whose gift was to understand the now.

He did not press her to voice it. Enough for this hour, that she was here and his.

Morgana rose, full, murky-spotted and less bright than formerly. So much had it been scarred. Tabby halted.

"Was it worth it?" she said. He heard the lingering anguish.

"The war, you mean?" he prompted.

"Yes." Her free arm rose. "Look there. Look everywhere—around this globe, out to those suns—death, maiming, agony, mourning, ruin—losses like that yonder, things we've cheated our children of—to make a political point!"

"I've wondered too," he confessed. "Remember, though, we did keep something for the children that they'd otherwise have lost. We kept their right to be themselves."

"You mean to be what we are. Suppose we'd been defeated. We nearly were. The next generation would have grown up as reasonably contented Imperial subjects. Wouldn't they have? So had we the right in the first place to do what we did?"

"I've decided yes," he said. "Not that any simple principle exists, and not that I couldn't be wrong. But it seems to me—well, that which we are, our society or culture or what you want to name it, has a life and a right of its own."

He drew breath. "Best beloved," he said, "if communities didn't resist encroachments, they'd soon be swallowed by the biggest and greediest. Wouldn't they? In the end, dead sameness. No challenges, no inspirations from somebody else's way. What service is it to life if we let that happen?

"And, you know, enmities needn't be eternal. I daresay, oh, for instance, Governor Saracoglu and Admiral Cajal had ancestors on opposite sides at Lepanto." He saw that she didn't grasp his reference. No matter, she followed his drift. "The point is, both strove, both resisted, both survived to give something to the race, something special that none else could have given. Can't you believe that here on Avalon we've saved part of the future?"

"Bloodstained," she said.

"That wasn't needful," he agreed. "And yet, we sophonts being what we are, it was unavoidable. Maybe someday there'll be something better. Maybe, even, this thing of ours, winged and wingless together, will help. We have to keep trying, of course."

"And we do have peace for a while," she whispered.

"Can't we be happy in that?" he asked.

Then she smiled through moonlit tears and said, "Yes, Arinnian, Chris, dearest of all," and sought him.

Eyath left Gray before dawn.

At that hour, after the night's revel, she had the sky to herself. Rising, she captured a wind and rode it further aloft. It flowed, it sang. The last stars, the sinking moon turned sea and land into mystery; ahead, sharp across whiteness, lifted the mountains of home.

It was cold, but that sent the blood storming within her.

She thought: *He who cared for me and he who got me share the same honor. Enough.*

Muscles danced, wings beat, alive to the outermost pinion. The planet spun toward morning. *My brother, my sister have found their joy. Let me go seek my own.*

Snowpeaks flamed. The sun stood up in a shout of light.

*High is heaven and holy.*

# POUL ANDERSON

Poul Anderson is one of the most honored authors of our time. He has won seven Hugo Awards, three Nebula Awards, and the Gandalf Award for Achievement in Fantasy, among others. His most popular series include the Polesotechnic League/Terran Empire tales and the Time Patrol series. Here are fine books by Poul Anderson available through Baen Books:

## THE GAME OF EMPIRE

A *new* novel in Anderson's Polesotechnic League/Terran Empire series! Diana Crowfeather, daughter of Dominic Flandry, proves well capable of following in his adventurous footsteps.

## FIRE TIME

Once every thousand years the Deathstar orbits close enough to burn the surface of the planet Ishtar. This is known as the Fire Time, and it is then that the barbarians flee the scorched lands, bringing havoc to the civilized South.

## AFTER DOOMSDAY

Earth has been destroyed, and the handful of surviving humans must discover which of three alien races is guilty before it's too late.

## THE BROKEN SWORD

It is a time when Christos is new to the land, and the Elder Gods and the Elven Folk still hold sway. In 11th-century Scandinavia Christianity is beginning to replace the old religion, but the Old Gods still have power, and men are still oppressed by the folk of the Faerie. "Pure gold!"—Anthony Boucher.

## THE DEVIL'S GAME

Seven people gather on a remote island, each competing for a share in a tax-free fortune. The "contest" is ostensibly sponsored by an eccentric billionaire—but the rich man is in league with an alien masquerading as a demon . . . or is it the other way around?

### THE ENEMY STARS

Includes for the first time the sequel to "The Enemy Stars"; "The Ways of Love." Fast-paced adventure science fiction from a master.

### SEVEN CONQUESTS

Seven brilliant tales examine the many ways human beings— most dangerous and violent of all species—react under the stress of conflict and high technology.

### STRANGERS FROM EARTH

Classic Anderson: A stranded alien spends his life masquerading as a human, hoping to contact his own world. He succeeds, but the result is a bigger problem than before . . . What if our reality is a fiction? Nothing more than a book written by a very powerful Author? Two philosophers stumble on the truth and try to puzzle out the Ending . . .

# FALLEN ANGELS

Two refugees from one of the last remaining orbital space stations are trapped on the North American icecap, and only science fiction fans can rescue them! Here's an excerpt from *Fallen Angels*, the bestselling new novel by Larry Niven, Jerry Pournelle, and Michael Flynn.

\*   \*   \*

She opened the door on the first knock and stood out of the way. The wind was whipping the ground snow in swirling circles. Some of it blew in the door as Bob entered. She slammed the door behind him. The snow on the floor decided to wait a while before melting. "Okay. You're here," she snapped. "There's no fire and no place to sit. The bed's the only warm place and you know it. I didn't know you were this hard up. And, by the way, I don't have any company, thanks for asking." If Bob couldn't figure out from that speech that she was pissed, he'd never win the prize as Mr. Perception.

"I am that hard up," he said, moving closer. "Let's get it on."

"Say what?" Bob had never been one for subtle technique, but this was pushing it. She tried to step back but his hands gripped her arms. They were cold as ice, even through the housecoat. "Bob!" He pulled her to him and buried his face in her hair.

"It's not what you think," he whispered. "We don't have time for this, worse luck."

"Bob!"

"No, just bear with me. Let's go to your bedroom. I don't want you to freeze."

He led her to the back of the house and she slid under the covers without inviting him in. He lay on top, still wearing his thick leather coat. Whatever he had in mind, she realized, it wasn't sex. Not with her housecoat, the comforter and his greatcoat playing chaperone.

He kissed her hard and was whispering hoarsely in her ear before she had a chance to react. "Angels down. A scoopship. It crashed."

"Angels?" Was he crazy?

He kissed her neck. "Not so loud. I don't think the 'danes are listening, but why take chances? Angels. Spacemen. *Peace* and *Freedom*."

She'd been away too long. She'd never heard spacemen called *Angels*. And— "Crashed?" She kept it to a whisper. "Where?"

"Just over the border in North Dakota. Near Mapleton."

"Great Ghu, Bob. That's on the Ice!"

He whispered, "Yeah. But they're not too far in."

"How do you know about it?"

He snuggled closer and kissed her on the neck again. Maybe sex made a great cover for his visit, but she didn't think he had to lay it on so thick. "We know."

"We?"

"The Worldcon's in Minneapolis-St. Paul this year—"

The World Science Fiction Convention. "I got the invitation, but I didn't dare go. If anyone saw me—"

"—And it was just getting started when the call came down from *Freedom*. Sherrine, they couldn't have picked a better time or place to crash their scoopship. That's why I came to you. Your grandparents live near the crash site."

She wondered if there was a good time for crashing scoopships. "So?"

"We're going to rescue them."

"We? Who's we?"

"The Con Committee, some of the fans—"

"But why tell me, Bob? I'm fafiated. It's been years since I've dared associate with fen."

Too many years, she thought. She had discovered science fiction in childhood, at her neighborhood branch library. She still remembered that first book: *Star Man's Son*, by Andre Norton. Fors had been persecuted because he was different; but he nurtured a secret, a mutant power. Just the sort of hero to appeal to an ugly-duckling little girl who would not act like other little girls.

SF had opened a whole new world to her. A galaxy, a

universe of new worlds. While the other little girls had played with Barbie dolls, Sherrine played with Lummox and Poddy and Arkady and Susan Calvin. While they went to the malls, she went to Trantor and the Witch World. While they wondered what Look was In, she wondered about resource depletion and nuclear war and genetic engineering. Escape literature, they called it. She missed it terribly.

"There is always one moment in childhood," Graham Greene had written in *The Power and the Glory*, "when the door opens and lets the future in." For some people, that door never closed. She thought that Peter Pan had had the right idea all along.

"Why tell *you*? Sherrine, we want you with us. Your grandparents live near the crash site. They've got all sorts of gear we can borrow for the rescue."

"Me?" A tiny trickle of electric current ran up her spine. But . . . *Nah*. "Bob, I don't dare. If my bosses thought I was associating with fen, I'd lose my job."

He grinned. "Yeah. Me, too." And she saw that he had never considered that she might not go.

*'Tis a Proud and Lonely Thing to Be a Fan*, they used to say, laughing. It had become a *very* lonely thing. The Establishment had always been hard on science fiction. The government-funded Arts Councils would pass out tax money to write obscure poetry for "little" magazines, but not to write speculative fiction. "Sci-fi isn't literature." *That* wasn't censorship.

Perversely, people went on buying science fiction without grants. Writers even got rich without government funding. *They couldn't kill us that way!*

Then the Luddites and the Greens had come to power. She had watched science fiction books slowly disappear from the library shelves, beginning with the children's departments. (That wasn't censorship either. Libraries couldn't buy *every* book, now could they? So they bought "realistic" children's books funded by the National Endowment for the Arts, books about death and divorce, and really important things like being overweight or fitting in with the right school crowd.)

Then came paper shortages, and paper allocations. The science fiction sections in the chain stores grew smaller. ("You can't expect us to stock books that aren't selling." And they can't sell if you don't stock them.)

Fantasy wasn't hurt so bad. Fantasy was about wizards

and elves, and being kind to the Earth, and harmony with nature, all things the Greens loved. But science fiction was about science.

Science fiction wasn't exactly outlawed. There was still Freedom of Speech; still a Bill of Rights, even if it wasn't taught much in the schools—even if most kids graduated unable to read well enough to understand it. But a person could get into a lot of unofficial trouble for reading SF or for associating with known fen. She could lose her job, say. Not through government persecution—of course not—but because of "reduction in work force" or "poor job performance" or "uncooperative attitude" or "politically incorrect" or a hundred other phrases. And if the neighbors shunned her, and tradesmen wouldn't deal with her, and stores wouldn't give her credit, who could blame them? Science fiction involved science; and science was a conspiracy to pollute the environment, "to bring back technology."

Damn right! she thought savagely. We do conspire to bring back technology. Some of us are crazy enough to think that there are alternatives to freezing in the dark. *And some of us are even crazy enough to try to rescue marooned spacemen before they freeze, or disappear into protective custody.*

Which could be dangerous. The government might declare you mentally ill, and help you.

She shuddered at that thought. She pushed and rolled Bob aside. She sat up and pulled the comforter up tight around herself. "Do you know what it was that attracted me to science fiction?"

He raised himself on one elbow, blinked at her change of subject, and looked quickly around the room, as if suspecting bugs. "No, what?"

"Not Fandom. I was reading the true quill long before I knew about Fandom and cons and such. No, it was the feeling of hope."

"Hope?"

"Even in the most depressing dystopia, there's still the notion that the future is something we build. It doesn't just happen. You can't predict the future, but you can invent it. Build it. That is a hopeful idea, even when the building collapses."

Bob was silent for a moment. Then he nodded. "Yeah. Nobody's building the future anymore. 'We live in an Age of Limited Choices.'" He quoted the government line without cracking a smile. "Hell, you don't *take* choices off a list. You *make* choices and *add* them to the list. Speaking of which, have you made your choice?"

That electric tickle . . . "Are they even alive?"

"So far. I understand it was some kind of miracle that they landed at all. They're unconscious, but not hurt bad. They're hooked up to some sort of magical medical widgets and the Angels overhead are monitoring. But if we don't get them out soon, they'll freeze to death."

She bit her lip. "And you think we can reach them in time?"

Bob shrugged.

"You want me to risk my life on the Ice, defy the government and probably lose my job in a crazy, amateur effort to rescue two spacemen who might easily be dead by the time we reach them."

He scratched his beard. "Is that quixotic, or what?"

"Quixotic. Give me four minutes."

# THE BEST OF THE BEST

For *anyone* who reads science fiction, this is an absolutely indispensable book. Since 1953, the annual Hugo Awards presented at the World Science Fiction Convention have been as coveted by SF writers as is the Oscar in the motion picture field—and SF fans recognize it as a certain indicator of quality in science fiction. Now the members of the World Science Fiction Convention— the people who *award* the Hugos—select the best of the best: *The Super Hugos*! Included in this volume are stories by such SF legends as Arthur C. Clarke, Isaac Asimov, Larry Niven, Clifford D. Simak, Harlan Ellison, Daniel Keyes, Anne McCaffrey and more. Presented and with an introduction by Charles Sheffield. This essential volume also includes a complete listing of all the Hugo winners to date in all categories and breakdowns and analyses of the voting in all categories, including the novel category.

And don't miss *The New Hugo Winners Volume I* (all the Hugo winning stories for the years 1983–1985) and *The New Hugo Winners Volume II* (all the Hugo winning stories for the years 1986–1988), both presented by Isaac Asimov.

*The Super Hugos* • 72135-6 • 432 pp. • $4.99 ☐
*The New Hugo Winners Volume I* • 72081-3 • 320 pp. • $4.50 ☐
*The New Hugo Winners Volume II* • 72103-8 • 384 pp. • $4.99 ☐

Available at your local bookstore. If not, fill out this coupon and send a check or money order for the cover price to Baen Books, Dept. BA, P.O. Box 1403, Riverdale, NY 10471.

NAME: _____

ADDRESS: _____

_____

I have enclosed a check or money order in the amount of $_____

# GORDON R. DICKSON

Winner of every award science fiction and fantasy has to offer, Gordon Dickson is one of the major authors of this century. He creates heroes and enemies, not just characters in books; his stories celebrate bravery and virtue and the best in all of us. Collect some of the very best of Gordon Dickson's writing by ordering the books below.